"So you knew I'd be here?" she asked

"Yes," David admitted. "When the Old Man first mentioned your name I felt as if I'd been hit over the head. Anyway, I wanted to meet your fiancé." He paused. "He's old enough to be your father."

Elizabeth turned away from him despairingly, and he caught her hand. "Are you really the way you are because of a deprived childhood?" he asked.

"I know if I stay here being tortured by you I'll go mad," she retorted, evading his question.

"Tortured...." He savored the word, pressing his thumb into the palm of her hand.

"Don't!" she cried.

David watched her lips moving soundlessly, then as though tormented by them, he covered them fiercely with his own. Five long, pain-filled years might never have happened. Elizabeth melted with a wild abandoned air against his body.

MARGARET WAY

broken rhapsody

Harlequin Books

TORONTO • NEW YORK • LOS ANGELES • LONDON
AMSTERDAM • PARIS • SYDNEY • HAMBURG
STOCKHOLM • ATHENS • TOKYO • MILAN

Harlequin Presents first edition November 1982
ISBN 0-373-10549-5

Original hardcover edition published in 1982
by Mills & Boon Limited

CHAPTER ONE

THE final chords of the Debussy died away and a few seconds later the mellifluous voice of an announcer informed those who were not yet aware of it that they had been listening to a studio recital by the pianist Elizabeth Rainer.

'Beautiful, darling,' Gavin breathed in her ear. In reality he was very pleased it was over. Though it suited him perfectly to have a gifted fiancée, indeed he was very proud of her, classical music did little to engage his interest. What did interest him was the girl herself. He tightened his arm possessively around her and bent his smooth fair head to draw a lingering kiss across her mouth.

'*Beautiful!*' he repeated, this time his pleasure monumentally unfeigned. Elizabeth had a lovely mouth, cushiony and curving, a passionate mouth, exposing her true nature. Inevitably she would find out, and he would be the lucky man.

'I suppose from a purely technical point of view it was,' Elizabeth was saying, not allowing herself to be kissed very deeply.

'Don't be silly, darling. You're terribly hard on yourself, I'm afraid.'

'Because I never play well enough. It doesn't seem likely I ever will.'

'Good grief!' Gavin swept her troubled face with a glance. 'You *are* in a mood.'

'The Debussy,' she sighed.

'Does that invite trouble?' he asked archly, experiencing a wonderful protective feeling. Women

5

seldom affected him this way.

How could she answer? She might say, 'I'm compelled to play it, though it does nothing but unsettle me and make me unhappy.' She could even say, 'Tonight for some reason it's disturbed me unbearably.' She could never say what was in her mind.

'Well?' Gavin demanded, his smile concerned and indulgent. He was a handsome man something over forty and he was profoundly in love for the first time in his life. 'Of course, you arty types are notoriously highly-strung.'

'I suppose so.' Elizabeth breathed deeply, unmistakably melancholy. 'Would you like some more coffee?'

'The coffee will keep. I want to talk to you, young lady.'

'About what?' She let her head fall back against his broad shoulder, staring up at the radiant sky. It was a beautiful night full of stars and a soft sensuous breeze and her slender body felt too indolent to move. They were sitting out on the tiny, plant-filled terrace of her apartment. Dinner was over and Gavin, most certainly, was looking forward to a romantic interlude when right at that moment she felt it was hopeless.

'When are you going to marry me, darling?' he asked gently, right on cue.

'I thought we agreed to stay engaged a little longer.'

He buried his face in her shining, scented hair. 'You're not being fair to me, you know that.'

'You mean we don't sleep together?'

'Not that precisely, but most engaged couples do.'

'Can it be I don't really love you as you deserve?' she asked tentatively.

'Oh, for God's sake!' Momentarily Gavin felt unable to grapple with this mood. 'We're ideally suited. For months now we've been inseparable—though I have to admit there's some little thing at the back of your mind.'

'My miserable childhood,' she explained.

'About which you never speak.' Gavin had been an adored only child of mature parents.

'I daren't,' Elizabeth said. 'Terrible, isn't it?'

He took her hand, turned it palm over and kissed it passionately. 'All the more reason we get married and let me look after you.'

'Would you like that?' She leaned forward to kiss his cheek, shamed by her lack of ardour when Gavin was so good to her.

'Darling, I'd adore it,' he said. 'We'd be so good together. We could entertain a lot—we'd be expected to, actually. You're so beautiful, and there's your playing. Sir William thinks the world of you. He thinks you're marvellous—he's always telling me what a lucky man I am and marry you off quickly before you change your mind.'

Elizabeth smiled, thinking about Sir William Langley. 'And what about children?' They had never discussed it.

'Why, I've never really thought about it,' Gavin confirmed. 'I mean, you have your music and my career is very demanding, as you know. My mind has never really run along those lines. Actually, darling, children could be very disagreeable.'

'I would want at least two,' she told him.

'You'd *what*?' Gavin seemed inclined to laugh. He supposed women might want children, but

Elizabeth had the solitary air of a princess in a tower. 'They would all have to look like you, darling. Angels.'

'Don't tease me, Gavin. I'm serious.'

'Well then, darling,' he said mildly, 'anything you want. Personally I think I'm too old to start a family. I'm no longer in my thirties, sixteen years older than you.'

'But don't you know I've always liked older men?'

'I know you need one,' he said. 'Tell me about you. You never will.' His hand found her breast and he caressed it through the silk of her shirt.

'You know the story,' she murmured almost absently. Gavin never forced his attentions and she knew in her bones he would be an experienced and skilful lover, so why did she deny him, always? Never meet his desires. She was going to marry him, wasn't she? She never expected to experience again the sublime passion she had once known. Nor the suffering. She had repudiated all that.

'I know you went to live with relatives when you were seven,' Gavin prompted.

'Who didn't want me.'

'Could there be anyone who wouldn't want you?' Gavin said. 'You must have been a ravishingly pretty child.'

'Women sometimes find it hard to like pretty children when they're not theirs,' Elizabeth said quietly. She was thinking of Aunt Ruth who had never ceased to be affronted by her looks. 'Of course I had a cousin—that was a lot of the trouble. I think Jill hated me from the very first day I arrived. We were the same age and we could have been good friends, but Jill saw me as some

kind of a threat. Uncle Simon wanted to love me, I
think, after all, I was his sister's child, but he saw
clearly he couldn't allow any real closeness to
develop. Both Aunt Ruth and Jill are burdened
with very jealous natures.'

'But they did take you in?'

'They did,' Elizabeth agreed. 'A shame when I
could have gone to the nuns. They might have been
kind. I didn't know for ages there was money—
some money, anyway. I was always made to feel I
was a tremendous drain on modest resources.'

'So who paid for your piano lessons?' Gavin
asked with faint surprise.

'Uncle Simon until I was fourteen. Then
someone else came forward, an important person
in our town.'

'Now this part sounds interesting.'

'It's the fashion of the rich to sponsor the needy
and deserving,' she told him. 'I was summoned up
to the Big House to play. That was what we always
called it, the Big House. Apparently I played well
enough, and afterwards I was sent away to Sydney
to study. I was so pathetically grateful I practised
my little fingers to the bone. Every time I went
back for vacations I had to go up to the House to
show off my progress. They had to be sure the
money was being well spent. At nineteen I was
shunted off to Germany for two years. Now I'm
home, good but not good enough. I don't pretend.'

'But, darling, you're exceptionally accomplished—everyone says so. That Doctor feller—
what's his name?'

'Summerton. Yes, he's sweet to me, but one has
to be better than good. Inside I never had the

dedication. It's a very hard life, and lonely. I love what I'm doing, I don't think I could live without my music, but I want so much more. I want happiness, a family. It often seems to me happiness *is* a family. I don't want to keep travelling the world, living in hotel rooms, not getting to know anybody. Everyone thinks you're invited everywhere so everyone doesn't ask you. I want marriage, I guess, but I'm frightened.'

'I've noticed,' Gavin said dryly.

'I'm not frightened of you, Gavin,' she said, and gave him her rare, very sweet smile.

Surprisingly it made him frown. 'Has it ever occurred to you, you might see me as a father figure? You're a little foundling at heart, a lost child searching for security.'

'Another penalty of my childhood.' Elizabeth linked her hands together, the fingers trembling. 'No, it's not that, Gavin. I'm happy with you, safe and confident. You're handsome, charming and considerate. You're so at ease in your fashionable world. You're also very clever and ambitious. I heard someone say the other day that you were the likely successor to Sir William by the time he's ready to retire.'

'And who was that?' Gavin asked quickly, tilting her head back.

'Oh, that tall woman with the black hair,' she teased him.

'Angela?'

'That's right. The one who's very keen on you—says the most unforgivable things about me behind my back.'

'Listen to you!' He drew her back against him again. 'Angela is not bitchy.'

'Any woman is bitchy when she's jealous. Did you ever take her out?'

'Lots of times,' he said instantly, with such casualness it was apparent he didn't think it important. 'Angela is a very attractive woman, a good companion, but I never fell in love with her. That had to be with a honey-blonde almost young enough to be my daughter.'

'You're not sorry?'

'Look at me.' He put a hand to her face. 'I love you and I want us to get married right away. You're so magical—you don't know.'

'And you're much more than I deserve.'

His emotions pent up, Gavin kissed her, over and over, but instead of it leading to possession gradually he could feel her slipping away. Not the body, but the mind. It had never occurred to him that winning Elizabeth would be easy, but he was determined to have her. Under different circumstances, married, she would respond. He was so curious now about her childhood he would make some investigations himself. Previously he had only guessed at her background. She was everything he wanted, beautiful and gentle and refined, but somewhere along the line she had been very badly hurt. The sudden awareness that it could have been a man made him clutch her to him convulsively.

'Let yourself go, darling,' he said insistently. 'If you let yourself relax it will happen.'

Did he think she had never known love, whatever the outcome?

'*Please*, Gavin!' Attraction and true passion were not the same, could never be.

'You're such a little innocent,' he said, almost tenderly.

How do you know? Elizabeth only thought it, never said it. Why hurt Gavin with a past she had long buried?

'By the way, darling,' he chose to tell her then, 'Sir William expects us down at Langley at the weekend. He has a few guests to entertain, one of them pretty important to us, I understand. We have to woo him. It's the greatest good fortune that the old boy has taken to you the way he has. He's an arrogant old devil, as you know, but you seem to be able to make him laugh and any old excuse to get you to play for him. Music seems to be his only relaxation.'

'While yours is golf,' Elizabeth smiled, perfectly well aware that Gavin didn't give her playing a good deal of attention. Actually it suited her that he wasn't aroused by her music. That had all happened to her before when she had lived that other life.

'Well, there's a golf course at Langley,' Gavin was saying with pleasure. 'I might get a game in. You'll love the old place, old houses being your style. It's a not so typical English gentleman's residence, built in the middle of the last century, of course—Gothic influence, lots of arches. and towers, and there's even a little stone chapel in the grounds. While we're talking business, you can go for lots of long walks. Marion is bound to want to go with you. She's as mad as a hatter about gardens and you're so good not to allow her to think she bores you.'

'But she doesn't!' Elizabeth stood up quickly and smoothed back her hair. Gavin had pulled the pins out, now it floated down her back in a heavy curtain. 'I like her. She's a really nice person, Marion.

She's got a fine mind and above all she's so genuinely kind.'

'Most people think she's quite ratty,' Gavin pointed out pleasantly. 'I don't mind her myself. It's bleak comfort for a rich woman to be so distressingly plain. And to think the old devil still has women chasing after him! Not just for his money either, you realise. Yet for all he's accomplished, he never fathered a son.'

'Why don't you get him to adopt you?' Elizabeth suggested, giving vent to the wry humour Gavin seldom saw.

'Now what is that supposed to mean?' Gavin's rather heavy, handsome face looked slightly awestruck.

'It's a fact he thinks the world of you,' Elizabeth pointed out levelly.

'As a matter of fact he does.' Instantly Gavin regained his normal composure. 'Anyway, you'll come?'

'Of course. I'd love to.' Elizabeth turned around to him and held out her hand.

'All settled, then.' With them both standing, he embraced her. 'Bring something pretty with you for the evenings. You know how he likes us all to dress up. We'll go down on Friday evening and come back early Monday morning. Miss the traffic that way. Still mad at the world?'

'I haven't decided.' She looked up at him with iridescent green eyes.

'You have to decide about us, darling.' Gavin skeined his hand through her glorious mane of hair, forcing her to look up at him. 'We'll get married, and if you insist, we'll have children. Not at the beginning—don't inflict them on me at the start. I want you all to myself.'

'You believe in love and marriage.'

'I believe in you.'

'You don't know me yet, Gavin,' she pointed out seriously.

'That's because you won't talk to me. That's one of your troubles, young lady—you keep too many things bottled up. Your playing is full of fire and passion, yet in your personal life you need a real shaking up.'

'The first criticism.'

'No.' He closed his arms around her tightly. 'How can you be cold when you have the most beautiful mouth?'

'Then kiss me.' She offered him her mouth, wanting to forget everything. But never quite forgetting.

She was lying on her back in the garden with the white heads of the dandelions all around her when Aunt Ruth came to the back door clapping her hands imperatively.

'Elizabeth, come inside this minute!'

It never occurred to her to shout, 'Why?' as Jill would have done. She sprang up immediately, her hands shaking because she thought Jill might have told on her for sitting up half the night reading. Wasn't the electricity bill high enough?

As it happened, Jill had informed on her, but that wasn't the reason for Ruth Warren's terrifying anger.

'You've been complaining again,' she said bitterly.

'Complaining?'

'We know!' Aunt Ruth and Jill both shouted together.

'What an ungrateful girl you are!' Aunt Ruth accused her, sighting her down her long, thin nose. 'Haven't we done everything we possibly could for you? Taking you in, rearing you as our daughter. I was never consulted. This was what your uncle wanted—proof of what a good Christian he is when I've done all the rearing.'

'I know, Aunt Ruth,' Elizabeth said earnestly. 'Believe me, I'm very grateful.'

'And how do you show it? Not a word do you utter that doesn't show us up in a bad light. Complaining because Jill got the red dress.'

'No.' Elizabeth tried to defend herself, turning in the light so the gold of her hair flared.

'Yes, you did!' Jill screeched, in her rage looking like a little monkey. 'All you ever do is complain. You've got all the teachers feeling sorry for you. You think you're Cinderella, and I'm the ugly sister.'

'What's wrong, Aunt Ruth?' Elizabeth had to rest back against the wall, feeling the familiar sick sensation in her stomach.

'Mrs Courtland's secretary has just rung me,' Aunt Ruth replied angrily. 'You're to be at the house at three o'clock this afternoon, and take your music.'

'Whatever for?' Elizabeth scarcely knew to believe her ears.

'Don't be stupid, girl!'

Jill began to cry.

'They want to hear me play?' Elizabeth was confused—worse, frightened.

'Oh, you're all surprise now,' Aunt Ruth accused her, 'when you've been complaining to Miss

Thomas that we begrudge the money that's being spent on your music lessons.'

'I never did.' Elizabeth shook her head.

'Liar!' Jill shouted.

'That will do, Jill,' Aunt Ruth said sternly. 'If your cousin chooses to be underhand. I've always said green eyes were sly.'

That was daily life. Green eyes, honey hair and white skin, a smile that illuminated her serious little face as her mother's once had. A smile that made her uncle feel saddened and guilty. It was only on prizegiving night that Ruth ever made a pretence of liking the child.

'I've never spoken to Miss Thomas. . . .' Elizabeth began. If they would only *listen*!

'It's what I expected, after all,' Aunt Ruth said bitterly. 'You're underhand and conceited, and Miss Thomas has been filling your head with a whole lot of nonsense. It's my opinion you have a very heavy touch. In fact, I can't bear to be in the same room where you're playing. But *Miss Thomas* thinks you have some sort of ability. She's gone over our heads at your instigation and asked the Courtlands to hear you play. It's their practice to dispense favours, but the minute they hear you, they'll change their minds.'

'I don't want to go,' Elizabeth said.

'You should have thought of that,' Aunt Ruth said shortly. 'You can't *not* go. After all, the Courtlands are Royalty.'

'And you've got nothing to wear. All your clothes are terrible!' Jill shrieked.

'How can they be terrible when I bought them?' her mother snapped. 'Nothing could be more suitable than your white dress.'

So Elizabeth had worn her white dress, because she was going to be a tall girl, too tight and too short, a momentous rendezvous, for at fourteen years of age when such things rarely occur she fell violently in love at once and for ever.

Now, as Elizabeth was ready for bed, she stood at her window staring up steadily at the star-spangled sky. It was useless to entreat them when once she might have.

'David,' she said. 'Oh, David.' The terrible thing about the heart, there was no end to its yearning.

CHAPTER TWO

THE drive down in Gavin's Daimler was remarkably short and pleasant.

'Lovely time of the year this, isn't it?' Gavin remarked. It was early spring and the gardens were a glory of magnolia, camellia, azalea and rhododendron; a miraculous display that lifted Elizabeth's spirits to a pitch of great harmony.

'When we're married,' she said, 'we shall have a garden.'

'We shall have a gardener,' Gavin laughed. 'Apart from anything else gardens are something about which I know nothing.'

'I adore magnolias,' Elizabeth continued. 'I should plant lots of them. They're so beautiful they soften the heart.'

'Sensitive little thing, aren't you?' Gavin patted her hand. 'Don't worry, you'll be able to ramble on about gardens to poor old potty Marion. Even the old man. I understand he planned the whole layout at Langley. Quite a big area too, about fifty acres.'

'Lovely!' Elizabeth exclaimed, with a strong desire to see it.

'By the way,' Gavin added, 'I've got tidings of great joy. Angela is coming along as well. They're a woman short.'

'Just as I was feeling hopeful,' Elizabeth said ruefully.

'Don't foresee trouble where there'll be none,'

Gavin warned her. 'Every time Angela has spoken of you to me she's been most benign.'

'But tumorous all the same.'

'Darling!'

'Sorry.' Elizabeth turned her blonde head to smile at him. 'After all, you're no ordinary man. You have a great deal to offer a woman.'

For answer he gave a little groan. 'Please let me love you soon. It's unbearable wanting you the way I do and then have you lift yourself away from me as tremulous as a bird.'

'I want to be good for you, Gavin,' she said with such urgency that he seriously considered pulling right off the road.

'Then that's all that matters. Just please don't be afraid. Sometimes I suspect someone hurt you unbearably.'

'It doesn't matter at all.'

'*Who* did?' he persisted.

'I was just a girl. Very young,' she shrugged.

'Are you a virgin, Elizabeth?' he asked her, for the very first time.

'No.' She shook her head. She felt sick; her stomach churned.

'It was a long time ago?'

'Yes.'

'Was it force?' he asked quietly, conscious that somewhere inside she was sobbing.

'No.'

'What went wrong?'

'He married someone else.' The pain came to her so knifelike she almost doubled up.

'Ah, my poor little girl!' He looked at her pale profile, the golden hair she always wore in a Grecian knot. 'I've sensed this all along, yet I've always seen you as a virgin. The experience must have been unique.'

'It was.' She lifted her head, tears swimming in her brilliant green eyes. 'Do you mind dreadfully, Gavin?'

'I mind that you've been hurt—more, scarred. He must have been a cruel devil to have made such an impression on you?'

'Don't let's talk about it,' she said, her mind whirling and suddenly filled with the past. 'It's all over long ago.'

'Yet it was very much alive just now.' A pulse was beating in Gavin's left temple. 'Some time when we're in bed together, you're going to tell me all about it.'

Never, she thought. Never like it was. Her own voice whispering, so painfully young and eager . . . I love you, I love you, I love you. David had possessed her and she had never forgotten; lives that touched briefly, an ecstasy and a nightmare. The night before, her dreams had been filled with malevolent ghosts.

'Elizabeth?' Gavin queried.

'I'm sorry.'

'You'd gone off again to that place in your mind. A place it would seem you're not going to allow me to follow.'

'It has nothing to do with us,' she told him gently, 'and the reason I don't talk about it is that I don't want to spoil the times we have together. Anyway, you look great. I love that new jacket.'

'Just right for a weekend in the country, don't you think?' Gavin positively beamed at her.

'I daresay Angela will be moved as well.'

'Not to worry,' Gavin told her matter-of-factly,

'Angela means nothing to me.' He was all smiles and smoothly handsome, in every respect a man who was destined for high places. 'I can't help thinking she's been asked along for this mysterious V.I.P. of the old man's. She's actually rather good at a social gathering, and I suppose you could say handsome?'

'I suppose you could,' Elizabeth conceded with a sudden vision of Angela's dominant, brunette good looks and her immense chic. She supposed Angela must be thirty-five, but she made thirty-five look absolutely the best age any woman could be. There again, for better or worse, she was very keen on Gavin and apparently determined to get him regardless of a trivial little thing like an engagement. Angela was a smart woman and she bitterly resented Elizabeth, perhaps seeing that though there was a good deal of affection on Elizabeth's side, she was indisputably not madly in love.

They came on Langley by way of a private road, bordered on both sides by magnificent golden wattles that spread their fragrance over a great distance.

'How perfect!' Elizabeth exclaimed.

'Terribly common, and to be truthful they give me hay fever,' Gavin told her.

'Poor you!' Sometimes she thought the devil got into her enlisting her to have these little stabs at Gavin. He was generous, he was kind, he was definitely in her power, yet occasionally he irritated her dreadfully. Had she, in fact, chosen the right partner when he neither enjoyed her music nor saw the beauty and colour of the gloriously flowering trees? It even occurred to her from time to time that she was revenging herself on David. David, her first lover, only lover, endless lover. Would she ever forget him, and she wanted to desperately, but the thought of him lived on in her with a destructive intensity.

'Langley coming up!' Gavin's voice broke the silence, the pleasure on his face indicating that he was totally unaware of the deep currents inside her. 'One would have to be a millionaire to merely get invited here. The old man has been terribly secretive—I don't even know the chap's name. Tremendously wealthy, though, I understand.'

'And a bachelor?'

'I think so, otherwise why bring Angela along? Her first husband shot himself—did you know that?'

'Really?' Elizabeth was astonished and appalled.

'Oh, it was an accident. Rather bad luck.' In among the commiseration was a persistent note of cheerfulness. 'He left her nothing, of course, but she's managed splendidly. A fine woman, Angela, in many ways.'

'What was she like as a lover?'

Gavin glanced at her and did not reply.

'Seduction itself,' said Elizabeth.

'Well,' Gavin said contentedly, 'she was quite satisfied with me.'

'Vanity, vanity!'

'Vain I am not.' In fact Gavin spent many hours keeping himself so attractive. 'Anyway, you're the girl I love, as you know.'

'Why?'

'Don't be stupid!' Gavin drove slowly through the colonnaded driveway. 'You're everything I want, my dream girl.'

'You must see things in me others don't,' sighed Elizabeth.

Gavin raised his fair eyebrows and glanced at her. 'Darling, you really do need a break. I'm bound to point it out, because you've been rather moody lately.'

'The sorrow in my soul.' To balance her words Elizabeth smiled at him warmly. 'Don't worry, we're going to enjoy ourselves this weekend. The weather is beautiful and if the grounds are anything to go on, the house must be magnificent.'

'I'd like something different myself,' said Gavin. 'It must be terrible trying to *do* everything—the maintenance.'

'I imagine Sir William has a very generous staff.'

'You mean he works poor old Marion to death. Cheap labour.'

'Did no one ever want to do anything for Marion?' Elizabeth asked.

'Don't worry about Marion,' said Gavin. 'She's happy enough with her dogs.'

I cry for us, Elizabeth thought. All women. Marion left to wilt in the shadow of a domineering father, universally regarded as foolish when she ran a big household and was very good at it. No one took Marion seriously when she had allowed herself to be endlessly exploited.

Late afternoon sunlight filtered through the thick canopy of the trees and Elizabeth looked out over the emerald green sloping lawns. Away to her left was a huge ornamental lake with a graceful little bridge spanning its lily-strewn waters, and even as she stared a pair of black swans sailed composedly from under the wooden span towards the thick fringing of reeds.

'Swans!' she exclaimed, entranced.

'Peacocks too, my dear. Many's the itme they've startled me.'

Half hidden in the curve of the thickly wooded drive was a small stone building, picturesque, its walls almost covered in ivy.

'The chapel?' Elizabeth asked.

'No, just a little lodge. A trysting place if you like. It's very comfortable inside. I must take you there if we can't find a minute alone.'

Out of the corner of her eye Elizabeth saw movement, then a few seconds later two beautiful sable collies raced for the car like a target.

'Good God, I do hope they're going to stop!' Gavin took the wheel in a firm grasp.

'Aren't they beautiful!'

'If they jump up they'll scratch the car,' Gavin complained. 'Ah, there's Marion.'

'May I put the window down?' Elizabeth laughed.

'As far as I know they don't bite. Unpredictable dogs, all the same, collies.'

With the window down Elizabeth could hear Marion's surprisingly piercing whistle and with a nice sense of obedience, the flying collies immediately came to a stop and sat down, looking so intelligent and handsome that Elizabeth turned quickly to Gavin. 'Aren't we going to stop and say hello?'

'Oh no, I think we just need to wave.'

'I think we should—see, Marion is coming.'

'I was afraid of that,' Gavin sighed. 'Poor old Marion, she wears the most ridiculous clothes.'

'I daresay, but she's nice.' Elizabeth was already smiling, responding to Marion's shy wave. 'Look here, I'm going to get out.'

'You'll be asking for trouble,' he warned, 'those collies might jump you.'

'I'm not worried. They look so beautiful and dignified.' Elizabeth opened the car door and stood out on the drive and the collies came to her, tails wagging.

'Be careful!' Gavin warned cautiously. 'I never pat a strange dog if I can help it.'

Elizabeth laughed with pleasure, stroking a silken ear.

'Ah, there you are, m'dear!' Marion greeted her in her soft voice. 'Don't let those two get all over you.'

'We're making friends.'

'With great success,' Marion's plain face was pink and softened. 'They're usually very stand-offish.'

Out of politeness Gavin was obliged to join them, giving no hint of his mild impatience. 'Are we the first to arrive?' He shook Marion's outstretched hand.

'I suppose so, I don't know. The boys and I have been walking.'

'It must be wonderful for them to have all this space.' Both the collies were now nudging Elizabeth with their heads.

'Careful, darling,' Gavin warned. 'You'll get hair all over you.'

'Go on!' Elizabeth looked very unconcerned. 'What are their names?'

'Solomon and Sheba.'

'And titled as well!'

'Sir William here?' Gavin asked, becoming bored.

'He's in a horrid mood,' Marion breathed. 'Forgot some file or other. That's why I'm out with the dogs.'

'What did I tell you—batty!' Gavin murmured when they were continuing their journey up to the house.

'I don't suppose she has an easy time,' Elizabeth said defensively.

'Pray God I can answer the old man's questions,' said Gavin. 'Undoubtedly it will be my fault the file's missing.'

The first view of the house was entrancing, though to Elizabeth's eye it had a decidedly ecclesiastical look, with the verandahs in the upper and lower storeys enclosed externally by stone Gothic arches. 'Bit of a mixture, isn't it?' she commented. 'Gothic revival, neo-medieval and a dash of Scottish baronial thrown in.'

'The great Battle of the Styles,' Gavin agreed, 'but it's so tremendously substantial—almost a castle by present-day standards.'

Sir William wasn't on hand to greet them and Elizabeth found herself shown to her room by the caretaker's wife, a sensible woman who disregarded the vagaries of her employer's temper altogether.

'I hope you'll be comfortable, miss,' she said, carefully rearranging some pink camellias in a bowl.

'I'm sure I shall, the room is lovely.'

'Sir William said you were to have it. It's the nicest room in the whole wing and it has a beautiful view of the enclosed garden.'

'Are we the first to arrive?' Elizabeth asked, already positioned at the French doors, looking out.

'Except for the family, miss. The Whitneys are flying in with another guest and I understand Mrs Randall is driving down herself. Shall I bring you a cup of tea, perhaps? Sir William doesn't dine until eight.'

'That would be lovely, but I'll come down. I might even take a stroll around the garden until the light's gone. The camellias are superb.'

'To my mind the most beautiful shrub of them all, yet I suppose; roughly speaking, we'd have to call them trees. You'll find plenty here a good thirty feet tall. The camellia was Lady Langley's favourite flower—and how I miss her! A wonderful lady. I can never get settled in my mind she's gone.'

'I expect she was very fond of you as well,' Elizabeth said gently and with understanding, and the plump, little woman smiled, her glance brightening.

'I've always worked for the family, miss. I can scarcely remember when I didn't. Lady Langley was beautiful. A real aristocrat. When Sir William was at his worst, she simply behaved as though he wasn't there. It only took him ten minutes after that to get himself in hand. If only Miss Langley had inherited her mother's skills!' The little woman made a clucking sound of pity and turned about. 'Tea in ten minutes, miss. I'll set it up in the library. I doubt very much if you'll see Sir William before pre-dinner drinks. He's in what Miss Marion calls "one of his forbidding moods". Some file or other gone missing.'

And how would that affect Gavin? Elizabeth thought. She had never seen Sir William in one of his famous tempers, but apparently everyone else had. Even in a high good humour no one could deny that he was a very formidable man, one of the country's most renowned industrialists and chairman of the board of innumerable companies which operated great pastoral companies, coal-mines, oil companies, land and sea transport, real estate—Elizabeth had lost track.

A few moments later Gavin walked through the open door of her room and stretched out his arms to her. 'You'll never guess where old Frank put me. About a mile away. There'll be no Edwardian scurryings up and down the corridors here.'

'Then it looks like the Lodge after all.' Elizabeth lifted her blonde head for his kiss. 'I gather we're the first to arrive?'

'No, Angela's just checked in.' Gavin stepped purposefully to the door and shut it. 'You know, you've got a much nicer room than mine.'

'Now's certainly the time to complain.'

'If only we were married!'. Gavin gave a sincere groan. 'It's a bit too much putting me so far away. I mean, I *am* your fiancé.'

'An engagement is one thing, being married is another,' said Elizabeth. 'I imagine Sir William feels obliged to keep us all nicely separated. I'm not complaining anyway, it's a beautiful room. I've never slept in a fourposter in my life.'

'Is that so?' Gavin's blue eyes lit up. 'Then expect to find one in our very first home.'

Angela was actually waiting for them to take tea, so hung up on Gavin that she barely spared Elizabeth a second glance.

'Oh, I do love this place!' she settled her jet black head against a wing-backed chair and briefly closed her long dark eyes. 'The luxury and the comfort.

Where's poor old Marion? I haven't laid eyes on her.'

'Walking the dogs,' Gavin told her tolerantly. 'I scarcely like to mention it, but the old boy's in one of his moods.'

'Dear God!' Angela heaved an elaborate sigh, swelling her inclined-to-be-voluptuous bosom. 'What fun it's going to be! Who's the mystery guest, do you know?'

'Well. . . .' Gavin hesitated.

'I'm dying to know!'

'Whoever he is, he's damned important to Sir William,' Gavin frowned.

'We might just be able to take a turn around the garden,' said Elizabeth, putting her empty cup down.

'Then take one,' Angela suggested, sharply smiling. 'Gavin and I will stay here. There's so much I have to catch up on.'

'Besides, I've done enough walking for one day,' Gavin pointed out in the tone of a man who had a few worries on his mind. 'You don't really want to go, do you, darling?'

'Of course she does,' Angela said lightly. 'Remember what it was like when *you* were twenty-four?'

'Yes, Angela, I do,' said Gavin, rather annoyed. Once in the early days she had implied that Elizabeth was far too young for him, so he was quite ready for her when she decided to raise the point again.

Elizabeth took her leave of them and spent the next half hour strolling around part of the extensive grounds. Marion and the collies were still out, to add to her enjoyment, and Elizabeth reflected yet again how nice Marion was.

'Oh, it's lovely to be so free of tension!' Marion breathed, directing Elizabeth down a path lined with flowering peach. 'I think the most important thing is to be at peace.'

'You must have many responsibilities,' Elizabeth prodded her gently.

'I suppose so. I don't cope very well,' Marion said vaguely. 'I'm the most terrible disappointment to my father. Why I even look like I do still remains mysterious. My father is still a handsome man and my mother was an acknowledged beauty. I resemble no one.'

'Except yourself.'

'You say that as though it's important.' Marion turned to her in the twilight and Elizabeth saw a pleasant-looking middle-aged woman wearing an unbecoming loose garment and a strong look of anxiety.

'Well, it *is*!' Elizabeth insisted, trying to reassure her. 'I'm sure there are many things you can do, and if you don't want to be the big social hostess surely you don't need to be.'

'Obviously my father needs someone,' Marion said uncertainly.

'Then he might think of getting himself a very sophisticated wife.'

'*Elizabeth!*' Marion whispered, shocked.

'There are countless women after him,' Elizabeth pointed out lightly, which was exactly the truth.

'Married to *Father*?' Marion exclaimed as though the lucky person would have to be a madwoman.

'You just don't understand aggressive people. Some can give back as good as they get.'

'Like that Angela,' Marion said rather sharply. 'I don't care for her at all. She puts on such airs—always makes me feel like a servant in my own home.'

'Why don't you take the plunge and put her in her place?' suggested Elizabeth.

'I couldn't!' Marion moaned. 'If you want to know, Elizabeth, I'm so glad you're here.'

'So am I.' Elizabeth looked up at the spectacularly flowering spring blossoms.

'People take me for a fool,' Marion said. 'I know they despise me. Poor old frumpy Marion, no beauty, no brains. No one even wants me for my money—and Elizabeth dear, I'm very rich.'

'It should make you self-confident,' Elizabeth told her as they retraced their steps.

'It doesn't,' Marion said unhappily. 'I'm dreading this weekend. Father goes out of his way to confuse me in front of our guests.'

It was true. Sir William did have a cruel streak; Elizabeth had remarked it herself.

'Don't underrate yourself, Marion,' she said, and gently touched the older woman's hand. 'People tend to see us the way we see ourselves.'

'You're a sweet girl to care,' Marion murmured tremulously. 'I only wish I had something to offer. Only I'm the greatest disappointment. Father has never let me forget it, and Mother for all her kindness was quite bewildered by her only child. I know for a fact she was quite upset by my looks.'

'You've got good hair,' Elizabeth pointed out presently.

'It's always been a trouble.' Marion put up a quelling hand to her thick, curly mop. It had been ruthlessly restrained in a tight bun centre back.

'I believe it could look lovely if you had it well cut, and surely so much less trouble.'

'Don't go worrying about my appearance,' Marion smiled. 'I'm beyond redemption.'

'Would you come with me if I made an appointment for you at a good hairdresser's?' Elizabeth asked.

'What for, dear?' Marion blushed.

'Because you *should*, Marion. You owe it to yourself.'

Marion shook her head. 'Let's face it, dear, it's better for me to dress down than draw attention to myself.'

'Whatever for?' Elizabeth asked, startled.

'I don't want to give Father more areas to criticise.' For a moment the tears stood in Marion's eyes. 'I should have had a string of handsome brothers. Father does everything else properly.'

'You're a very cultured woman, Marion,' Elizabeth protested, both of them stopping so the collies could catch up with them. 'Very well read.'

'Nobody cares. In our house the only thing important is making money or for the daughter of the house to be handsome and a brilliant hostess. I've had endless years of humiliation, Elizabeth. Having my hair cut won't change that.'

'We'll have it done all the same.' Elizabeth found herself quivering with sympathy from head to foot. It was surprising, if Marion had so much money, that she stayed around to take it. A near genius, not surprisingly Sir William was troubled by his daughter's inadequacies, but there was no reason why Marion should be made to feel guilty all her life. Because Marion liked and trusted her Elizabeth experienced a fierce desire to help. They could go shopping. Marion's rather terrible loose garment did not conceal an overweight figure; Elizabeth had seen her in an equally terrible swimming costume and Marion was amazingly trim. Perhaps she was even frightened of discovering within herself some attraction. Obviously her childhood had exhausted her, and Elizabeth knew all about that. Progress, in fact if, she could manage it, given Marion's reluctance, would be slow.

With so much time on her hands Elizabeth bathed slowly, trying to ignore a curious nervousness. The bathroom was larger and lusher than anything she had ever seen, with an opulent circular bath, apricot carpet, lots of arched mirrors over the curving custom-made vanity, a chandelier dripping crystal, gold taps and fittings and what she really liked, a wonderful old stained glass window beneath which luxuriant ferns had been heaped.

'What's the matter with me?' she said aloud, scattering a few more pink bath salts into the fragrant water. Perhaps Marion had depressed her. She could always be relied upon for a sympathetic ear, but she already knew it wasn't Marion. For no good reason, her nerves were very sharply on edge as though she was poised on the brink of danger.

Slowly she stood up, reaching out for one of the luxurious apricot towels, then fitting it around her slender form. If she allowed herself, her nervous state could dissolve into real panic. But why? There was no logical answer for it. She knew she would be expected to play for Sir William's guests, but over the years she had developed considerable composure to cover her ever-present nerves. New people didn't bother her. She didn't suffer from shyness—besides, she knew the Whitneys quite well. Angela was a pain but not panic-forming, so she supposed she must be apprehensive about their mystery guest.

Back in the bedroom she sat down in front of the antique rosewood dressing table and started to brush her hair out. Her eyes were shimmering in the glowing light, pools of green against her white skin. She was uncertain now which dress to wear, the white or the green. Gavin had seen neither, but her heart didn't leap at the thought of his seeing her in either. She couldn't help herself, she sighed, and the hand holding her silver brush trembled.

Once she had seen herself through a lover's eyes, wanting to be beautiful, desirable, the blood racing through her veins like fire. Was there only to be one man in her life who could raise her responses to fever pitch? She knew it was true and momentarily she couldn't stand it. To have loved so deeply, so early—it had ruined her for ever.

She sat there taking measured breaths, trying to bring herself back to a state of calm. She didn't want to think of David, yet he seemed so very close, almost as though he were touching her. The very thought made her close her eyes, shivering with remembered rapture. What was it she and David had felt? A love so violent, so passionate, it was crazy, ill-starred.

In the end, she decided on the green to give her courage. It was a beautiful dress, deep as jade, a luxury dress because Gavin expected it, and in it she looked very elegant and self-possessed. Gavin's diamond and emerald pendant earrings swung against her cheeks and the necklace that accompanied them almost reached the shadowed cleft between her breasts.

'You must look affluent, darling,' Gavin had smiled at her. 'Besides, on you, emeralds are perfection.'

Gavin was her future—she had to keep telling herself that. It wasn't difficult. She was very fond of him. He would make a good husband and she was going to do everything in her power to make him proud of her and happy. Unlike Marion, she wasn't miserable in company. Now as she turned to the long mirror to stare at herself like a stranger she saw a cool blonde in a brilliant green dress. Her hair was parted in the centre, drawn into its usual immaculate coils. She looked expensive, exclusive, all over. She didn't look like herself at all.

Coming down the stairway, she could hear the clink of ice in glasses, the murmur of voices and curious emotions spurted up in her. This wasn't the only grand staircase she had walked. The one at Ravenswood was even grander, rising above black and white marble flooring, a wide first landing where the stairway divided at right angles leading to the gallery and the upper reaches of the house. Ravenswood. Instinctively she shut her mind on it. She might look as if she belonged in such a place now; she hadn't then. The odd little orphan with the saving talent.

The great chandelier in the entrance hall looked magnificent at night. Again Elizabeth caught a glimpse of herself in a tall, gilded mirror. Unfamiliar, a role. Then, quite suddenly, Sir William came out of the drawing room to greet her, his handsome, rather brutal face surprised into showing his pleasure.

'Ah, Elizabeth, there you are!'

It was simply a question of gliding towards him and receiving his kiss on her cheek. 'Good evening, Sir William. I'm so glad you invited me.'

'If Gavin's not careful I tell you I'll take you off him.' In a high good humour he slipped his arm around her narrow waist and drew her into the drawing room, a possessive gesture that guaranteed her entrée into his rarefied world. 'You know everyone, my dear, except my godson.'

Elizabeth thought her lips parted in a moan. *David.* The shock of it couldn't be controlled. Sir William was still holding her, performing the introductions, while all the time she thought she was going to lose consciousness.

'Miss Rainer.'

'No, really, David—*Elizabeth*,' Sir William laughed.

Had she given him her hand? He was holding it tightly while the world receded, then came back again. *David.* Impossible. God, it was too strange.

'I feel I know you,' he said in his beautiful, black velvet voice. 'You're just as perfect a creature as Bill told me.'

The blood rushed back inside her skull and she moved a little so the full skirt of her silk taffeta dress rustled. 'The fact is I'm as human as everybody else.'

Look away from his eyes, she thought, and never, *never* look into them again.

'Elizabeth is the most wonderful pianist,' Sir William told him. 'You're going to hear her later. Now, what about a drink, my dear?'

She nodded and walked towards Gavin, her legs shaking.

'Darling, you look beautiful.' Gavin, too, kissed

her, his blue eyes fixed on her with an element of worry. She did indeed look beautiful, but rather fey—or maybe distraught. He saw it with a terrible, protective clarity, holding her hand while she sank like a lily on to the sofa.

'Lovely dress, Elizabeth,' Angela observed. 'Is it an original?'

Across the intervening space Ellie Whitney smiled at her, a smile as comforting as a squeeze on the hand.

Somehow she got through the pre-dinner drink period. The men were already talking business, prepared to talk it for ever, and only Angela dared interrupt them, her own business sense so remarkable she had won herself a place in the world of privilege.

'I'm convinced, David, you could have an exhilarating life at my right hand.'

Even as Sir William's comment pierced the women's chatter, Elizabeth glanced at Gavin and saw the shock on his face that was quickly buried. Gavin believed, was *encouraged* to believe, he was Sir William's top executive.

'I never even knew David was invited,' Marion was confiding in an undertone. 'Of course it's just the sort of thing Father *would* do.'

'He can't take a chance on being without the right successor.' Ellie Whitney leaned forward, flashing Elizabeth a sympathetic look. 'Gavin, of course, is assured of a very high place, but for some reason I don't think Sir William finds him positive enough for the top job. His very niceness could be a disadvantage. David is very young, thirty-one, but he's no novice at big business. In fact Jack tells me his ability is astonishing. He's been running *his* family businesses since he's been little more than a boy. I suppose it's an advantage to be born the son of a millionaire, but they're not all chips off the same block. Jim tells me David Courtland has already built up a formidable reputation. He's a fellow director on Magnus Maritime and the Clayton Group. I believe Oakfields nearly went under, but for his recommendations. Matthew Oakfield appointed him as his number two.'

Elizabeth sat there speechless, thinking the whole world was collapsing around her ears. No one should be made to suffer so badly twice. If somehow David became part of Sir William's organisation she could no longer remain engaged to Gavin. It was even possible Gavin would discover they had known each other before.

'You look upset, Elizabeth,' Marion said suddenly.

'Never!' She made a great effort to smile.

Angela looked at them all, exasperated. 'If anyone asked for my personal recommendation, I'd give it to Gavin. For over a year now Sir William has allowed him to think he's well in the running.'

'And so he is,' Ellie Whitney said soothingly. 'David could well tell the Old Man to go to hell. What's more, I could just hear him saying it. Believe me, he's in no fear of the Great Man.'

'Unlike the rest of us,' Angela said with a faint jeer. 'Anyway, he's as handsome as the devil himself. His looks alone should earn him a standing ovation.'

At dinner it pleased Sir William to place Elizabeth beside David while David himself sat on Sir William's right.

'It's been a long time since you've sat down to this table.'

'Yes, it is,' David answered after the faintest pause.

'And it gives me great pleasure to have you here,' Sir William added forcefully. 'You can stand with me, David, or serve elsewhere.'

'This isn't the boardroom, Bill,' David Courtland said smoothly.

'You know the kind of man I am.' Sir William didn't seem at all put out. 'I can't pretend I don't want you. I always admired and respected your father, and I know we both hoped one day you would join me.'

'Thank you for your confidence in me.' David Courtland's black eyes swept the table, so brilliantly perceptive that Gavin spilt a drop of his wine on the tablecloth. The Old Man would appoint a number two over his dead body!

The meal took nearly two hours, starting with a superb crab bisque, roast stuffed shoulder of lamb served with a mushroom and avocado pilaff, glorious home-grown strawberries and cream, an obviously gourmet chocolate torte and a selection of cheeses.

It was perfectly prepared and served, yet it was irrevocably spoiled for Elizabeth. If the truth had been told, she wanted to escape with her life. It was agony on the grand scale, sitting beside David, trying to go through the functions of a good guest. Afterwards she resolved to tell Gavin the truth. She had already confessed the small part David had played in her life, her lover.

'Drink up, Elizabeth,' Sir William advised. 'It's not every day you'll taste a wine like that.'

'Really something,' Jack Whitney agreed, and

began to talk about a particularly luscious dessert wine he had recently added to his prodigiously well stocked cellar.

Angela broke in with her well informed comments and the name of a big, dry red that offered exceptional value.

'I'm looking forward to hearing you play,' David told Elizabeth, impaling her with a few words.

Afraid she might be giving herself away, she turned to him, discovering he hadn't changed at all except to look older, harder, better. 'What kind of music do you like, Mr Courtland?' she asked.

'At the moment I'm thinking of a little Debussy waltz. More an encore type of thing. *La plus que Lente*—do you know it?'

I hate you, her eyes told him. I hate you for your cruelty and for coming back into my life.

'Why, surely you play it often?' Gavin nodded approvingly when he wanted to take Courtland by the throat. 'You included it in your last recital, remember?'

'Perhaps you'll play it for me later?' David goaded her. They were staring into each other's eyes, and even now after everything Elizabeth was devouring those well remembered features, noting the changes. The brilliant, faintly reckless air was gone. Here was a man who had his life, his thoughts and his feelings better organised than anyone else one would know. The almost awesome good looks had hardened into a different mould, as faultless as ever but wholly sombre, wholly stern; blue-black hair, olive skin, hollow planes, brilliant black eyes, slanted brows, lashes that were thickly emphatic. The look of high-mettled youth, the vivid smile, the sweetness about the sculptured mouth was gone. David Courtland looked a powerful and dominant man, the natural successor to Sir William Langley. It caused her great distress.

Following their host's usual pattern, the men retired with Sir William to the library and the women were left to entertain themselves.

'One of the more unpleasant aspects of big business,' Ellie moaned. 'I sometimes think dear old Bill has no respect for a woman's judgment at all.'

'Steel yourself to it,' Angela advised. 'What I can't understand is how a man like that isn't married?'

'But he *is*.'

Angela turned on Elizabeth quickly, looking perplexed. 'Then where the devil is she? And in any case, how do *you* know? I'm sure you didn't exchange more than a dozen words over dinner.'

'Actually,' Marion said very quietly, 'David's wife is dead. She was killed in a car smash about two years after they were married—a great tragedy. His mother was killed too. They were both in the car.'

'*Elizabeth?*'

Vaguely Elizabeth heard Ellie's voice calling her, then her head was thrust down with Ellie's small, firm hand pressed down on her nape.

Melanie killed? Mrs Courtland? None of it had lost its power to haunt her.

'Dear girl!' Marion was saying.

'Hold on to her or she'll flake out on the carpet.' Angela's voice was fascinated and impatient.

Gradually the feeling passed and, aware that Elizabeth was reviving, Ellie removed her grip. 'How are you now, Elizabeth?'

'I'm sorry.' Elizabeth lifted her head.

'I hope you're not coming down with something,' Marion said, concerned, taking Elizabeth's limp hand and chaffing it with her own.

'Could be,' Elizabeth murmured, lying.

'What about a brandy?' Ellie stood up, grateful to see the colour come back into Elizabeth's pale cheeks.

'It's all right, Ellie. The feeling has gone away now.'

'I hope so.' Marion sat down beside Elizabeth on the long sofa. 'How did you know David was married?'

'I must have read it.' How many lies would she be obliged to fabricate?

'David never speaks about it,' Marion said. 'He was shocked out of his mind.'

Elizabeth nodded her head but could not reply. The news had come as a terrible blow to her as well. She would have to hold back her tears until later. Mrs Courtland had been kind to her in the early days, but after David had looked at her the kindness had been abruptly withdrawn. David Courtland would never have been allowed to marry a wretched little orphan and in the end he was true to his training.

While Marion and Ellie were fussing over her, the men returned, instantly perceiving something was wrong.

'Elizabeth is a little off colour,' Ellie explained.

Gavin moved towards her instantly, torn between concern and the stricken feeling his fiancée was about to disappoint the Old Man.

'Really, I'm all right,' Elizabeth assured them all with a smile.

'Good,' Sir William gave a pleased nod. 'David here is anxious to hear you play the piano.'

'The Debussy.' He affected a charming smile to cover the terrible cruelty.

Elizabeth knew exactly what he was doing to her. She even knew he was dangerous, more so now than he had ever been in the past. But there she wasn't the helpless little girl she had once been, inexperienced, insecure, beholden to the mighty Courtlands. She stood up gracefully and walked to the big Steinway grand Sir William had only just recently installed at Langley.

'Especially for you, my dear,' he had told her over the phone, instantly comparing her ability with his daughter's terrible efforts. Poor Marion! She had perhaps thought it a thousand times.

'Lid up, my boy,' Sir William called to his godson smilingly. 'This girl can really make the piano sound.'

'You *do* know how to make the Old Man happy,' David told her under cover of the happy sprinkling of applause. 'When I look back I realise how you always seemed to be able to charm the men.'

'Go away, David,' she said softly. 'Go away to where you belong.'

'And leave my godfather to will everything to *you*?'

It took superhuman strength to sit down on the glossy, ebony bench. Life was inexorable, grinding, fate. As much as he hated her, how could he possibly believe Sir William had anything but the most superficial interest in her?

Elizabeth closed her eyes, tilted her head back, trying to clear her clouded mind of its pain and bitter disillusionment.

'I think I'd like to sit over here watching you,' David said, drawing the words out, deliberately disturbing, exciting.

He can't touch me if I close the door on everything but my music, she thought. It has meant everything to me; sanity, control. Even with her eyes shut she could see his aggressions, sense the manic hostility. Mrs Courtland had paid her to go away, suggested Germany, a fine teacher. She recalled that wonderful man, his silver hair and his blue eyes, the way he had demanded the absolute best of her. . . . Pain, what is that? Broken hearts, love affairs. You have been given a gift you have come to me to refine. Play, Elizabeth, *play*. Since your heart has known suffering your music will have depth. You have a pure, spiritual quality, but you also have passion. You *will* bear your life, give other people happiness.

She heard the Professor's words, a great teacher and a healer, so gradually peace engulfed her. Her hands on the keys was the only power she had ever known.

Fifteen minutes later, when she had returned to her body, Sir William came to her and kissed her, the light of the genuine music-lover in his eyes. 'I judge that your finest performance yet!' He straightened and put his hands on her shoulders. 'What a wonderful thing it is for a woman to have such an accomplishment. You'll pass it to your children.'

The others were showing their pleasure, David with a smooth compliment, though she knew in her heart he had willed her to mediocrity. He who had once taken her body, all her heart and her mind had no comfort to give her but humiliation when he was ready. Yet here they were pretending to be strangers—a game with no wisdom in it.

Afterwards she and Gavin walked in the garden for a short while, merging with the shadows while Gavin gave vent to his anxieties.

'In all probability the Old Man is only testing me,' he said uncertainly. 'No wonder people hate him. He has a reputation as the most devious old devil in the business. I mean, who is this Courtland man anyway? He hasn't really proved himself. He's just the son of a very wealthy man. I didn't even know the Old Man *had* a godson. I wonder if there's any connection between him and Courtland Pastoral Corporation?' Gavin sounded blustery, talking more to himself than Elizabeth.

'I think he's the overall vice-chairman,' she told him.

'What?' Gavin's voice cracked.

Oh, my God! Elizabeth thought. She would have to think before she broke into speech. 'I believe he said he was. Or it might have been Ellie.'

'I don't understand this,' said Gavin. 'It seemed to me it was worrying you having him beside you at dinner.'

'He's not a comfortable man,' Elizabeth returned rather flatly.

'I've begun to fear him already.' Gavin tightened his hold on her arm. 'In fact it would pay me to prepare some kind of strategy, sound out some of the other directors. The Old Man seems determined to have him on the team, but I'm reasonably confident I could expect a lot of support if it came to a battle. Then there's you. The Old Man expects his top men to have the right women. This Courtland character, I'm willing to bet, is a lady-killer. I

can spot it head on. Women spend their entire time
flinging themselves at men like that.'

'His wife was killed tragically,' Elizabeth said,
rather surprised her voice didn't tremble.

'Never——' Gavin stared at her pure profile. 'I
had no idea.'

'Marion told us when you were in the library.'

'That *is* a surprise.' Gavin sounded thoroughly
startled. 'For no particular reason I was convinced
he had never cared for a woman in his life. There's
something hard in him—unrelenting. I suppose in
a way, he's a man after the old devil's own heart.'

Still vaguely grumbling, Gavin walked her back
towards the house, pausing just beyond the pool of
light to take her in his arms.

'I think somebody's watching us,' Elizabeth said,
more intuitively than actually seeing.

'Who cares? You're mine and I want everyone
to know.'

For the first time ever, Gavin's kiss bruised her
mouth, his anxieties finding a release in faint violence. To an onlooker it would have looked a very
passionate embrace, only Elizabeth couldn't control the sick feeling inside her; being accosted by a
past she had thought long behind her. Yet the past
was always there, the old wounds that never really
healed.

'Darling,' there was a faint trembling in Gavin's
strong arms, 'when are you going to give yourself
to me? All this is just wasting time. I love you and
I want you. I need the comfort of your body. Ah,
hell. . . .'

Yield, Elizabeth thought. Yield, let him have
what he wants.

'Are you really so cold?' Irrationally Gavin's

resentments were now directed at her.

'I find it hard to show my emotions.'

'You showed them once,' Gavin pointed out insultingly.

'I knew you'd finally get around to saying that,' she said bitterly. 'I should never have told you.'

'You know you had to,' Gavin said with tired patience. 'I guess having Courtland here has unsettled me. In more ways than one he presents a dilemma.'

With an electric sense of expectancy Elizabeth looked away across the broad lawn, to see David Courtland watching them. Her face flushed and her heart gave a sudden painful lurch.

'I don't know why, exactly,' Gavin said, 'but that man is interested in you. You haven't met him before, have you?'

Now was the time to say it, but she didn't. Gavin was already feeling hounded and beset. 'Why ever would you ask that?' she gave a quick, little laugh.

'Okay, I know it's ridiculous. Of course you're a very beautiful young woman, but all the same I can't think he likes you. Rather the reverse. There's an absence of all tolerance in his eyes.'

'Let's pretend he's not here.'

Her words and the way she said them gave Gavin a passing elation. He put his arm around her waist, the flag of ownership, and walked her slowly back to the house.

Damn Courtland! He would give anything in the world to know what the Old Man was really planning.

CHAPTER THREE

ELIZABETH woke early with the birds in full-throated chorus. Her eyes travelled slowly around the room, remarking the assemblage of beautiful furnishings and objects. It was a very subtle colour scheme, celadon, white and gold, and was remarkably restful, yet rest had not come to her.

The night had been full of fragmented dreams, oddly real, oddly naked. She did not want to get up, face the day, but she had to. There was no pleasure in a lie-in, savouring the birdsong and her beautiful surroundings; there was too much on her mind.

She threw back the bedclothes and stood up, a small pulse throbbing at the base of her throat. If she didn't panic, she could get through this weekend. For a short time she would be treading on glass, the cuts going deeper and deeper, then she would move away. It would be impossible to live in the same world as David Courtland, Gavin's devoted wife. Yet there remained the possibility David would reject whatever enticements Sir William was bent on offering. Only that would save her. By nature a fighter, so affected was she by the thought of having to see David constantly that she had already accepted being driven away; accepted the break-up of her engagement. Gavin's career lay with Langley enterprises and she considered with distress that he couldn't be expected to give his life up and follow her eagerly. Angela would be there to pick up the pieces.

Under the shower she eased her headache, then she dressed quickly in narrow white pants and a yellow crêpe shirt and walked out along the enclosed verandah. There was absolutely no one about, only a scene to delight her. Camellias and azaleas were flowering everywhere, in the garden and out of ornate pots in an endless array of colour and varieties. The sight of them she received gratefully, passionately desiring relief. Even now her mind could hardly touch on anything but David's reappearance in her life. It was a fantasy and an agony.

A few minutes later she emerged into the glorious morning light with the birds keeping up their continuous orchestrations. What harmony! she thought, astonished. A thousand little throats heralding the new day, the wondrous gaiety and the joy, and not a note out of place. She stopped and looked back at the house, finding it irrepressibly romantic. A property like this would cost millions, yet Sir William Langley only used it as a country retreat; somewhere to slip away and entertain his guests. Sunlight glinted off the leaded, diamonded windows, giving the impression of a hundred eyes watching her.

She turned and ran, plain common sense abandoning her. It was terrible to feel intimidated and pinned down by fate. Was she never to know the joys of ordinary life without all the drama that had come her way? She could not even remotely grasp why so many sinister things had happened to her. Wasn't it enough to have her parents swept away from her, left an orphan, convulsively crying herself to sleep night after night?

Where *was* God? As a child she had sat looking up at the sky, imploring him, calling out her mother's name. But her mother never came back and in her place, Ruth. She never thought of Ruth but her face didn't sadden, like an invisible cloud over the sun. Ruth had been particularly cruel about David, but at least Ruth had warned her.

She ran for a long time until she felt giddy and lightheaded. She ran like a child demanding release, her long hair freed and streaming out behind her in a golden, luxuriant tide. The ancient peacefulness of Nature, the solace it offered. The trees were interlocking now, century-old giants, screening the brilliant flood of the sun, and still running she was caught and held with a strange, lost cry dying in her throat.

'Elizabeth.'

She would respond to his voice in her grave.

'Now isn't this all too strange!'

She threw up her head with her soft hair falling all around her face. 'I never. . . .'

'All hail!' He was staring down at her with contemptuous intensity and boldness. 'Incredibly, Elizabeth. Looking different, an imperious young beauty, triumphant, with a rich fiancé on her arm. Sweetheart,' he said jeeringly, 'I just knew I could never finish my life without seeing you.'

'I never knew,' she whispered. My God, please help me.

'Does it hurt like hell seeing me?' he demanded, and actually shook her with ruthless strength.

'Please, David!' she begged.

'*Does* it?'

'Yes.'

The hard, handsome mouth curved sardonically.

'You never knew I was to be a guest in this house?'

'No.'

'I don't accept that at all.'

'It's true.' She threw back her head at his harshness, her windswept hair like blazing silk in the dappled sunlight. 'You couldn't possibly think I'd want to see you?'

'What's so strange about that?' His eyes swept her face, brilliantly insolent. 'I mean, you're the strangest, cruellest, out-and-out crazy girl I ever knew.'

'Of course I am,' she agreed a little wildly, 'but does it matter now? We hurt each other as much as we were capable long ago.'

'Did we?' His face visibly tightened into a daunting mask. 'I guess you were never very intelligent.'

'Please let me go, David. You're hurting me.'

'Outraged?' His hands tightened. 'Maybe you're about to be punished five years too late. Where did you go, Elizabeth?'

'It doesn't matter,' she swallowed with difficulty, not even caring in her anguish if he killed her.

'My dear, dear Elizabeth,' he said softly, 'how pleased I am to see you again.'

'What do you intend to do?' She met his eyes steadily and saw a furtive admiration that was quickly spent.

'Leave you wondering.'

'You can't hurt me,' she said bravely, like a child, her skin bereft of colour, extremely white.

'Does your fiancé know you're not a virgin?'

Now she flushed, her colour deepening. 'We've discussed it.'

'And is he already in your bed?'

'He's not your kind of man, David,' she said, unquelled by his look.

'You mean he doesn't give way to his shameful emotions? No one could be engaged to you, Elizabeth, and not anticipate a blissful marriage. I wish him much pleasure.'

'Then I may go?' She turned her head to glance meaningfully at the steely fingers that still held her, and as she did so his raised knuckles grazed her smooth skin. Burning it . . . burning . . . the electric tingle of danger and excitement.

'No, Elizabeth, you may not.' The chaotic response sparkled in the depths of his own eyes. 'It seems now I'm in the ironic position of being able to oust your fiancé. With *Sir William*, of course.'

'An unfair advantage.' She was stung into vindicating Gavin. 'Gavin is a good man.'

'To my mind not good enough.'

'As splendidly arrogant as ever! How would you know, David?' It was no use struggling. His hold on her was implacable.

'My dear girl, though the poor fool may be very deeply infatuated with you, it shouldn't prevent you from seeing he's not tycoon material.'

'And you are?' she asked with false calm.

'I would venture to suggest Sir William thinks so. Hard luck, baby.'

'So you mean to join his organisation?'

'Ah yes, my love,' he drawled, obviously enjoying himself. 'Actually you decided me. My life has been empty, you have no idea. I want to fill it with——'

'Cruelty?'

'You should know. In that field, you're decidedly a great artist.'

'Dear God!' Elizabeth almost sagged against him. It was obvious to her now that David was going to use any method at all to humiliate her. Pride was a deadly sin, and he was a very proud man.

'You know, one of the things I always admired about you, Elizabeth,' David told her, 'you were always ready to move up to bigger and better things.'

It was plainly an insult, but she didn't react. 'I don't have to listen to you, David.'

'So why are you standing here, golden head bent like a victim?' He smiled down at her, his eyelids half covering his brilliant black eyes. 'You want to join the big time, isn't that true? Strange, when you could have had me. I was fairly rich, even then. But you could hardly sacrifice a great talent to become a little housewife. The whole world was waiting. What happened, Miss Rainer, not good enough?'

'I never wanted what you thought at all.'

'Liar.' He shifted one hand and pressed up her chin. 'Didn't you always want to be a celebrity? Forever striving for perfection. A formidable trait, that. "Listen to her," my grandmother used to say. "Just *listen*, David. I'm sure we're all going to be very proud of Elizabeth one day!"'

Tears were in her eyes, but she stared back at him. 'Your grandmother was very kind to me. The only one, always.'

'The rest of us saw through you, that was the difference,' he jeered.

'The rest of us?' Her voice was very young and stern. 'You mean your mother.'

The planes of his face tightened into a frighten-

ing mask. 'Don't mention my mother, Elizabeth,
or I might strike you.'

'Not for the first time, I think.'

'You gave me lots of rights over you.'

She felt the heart within her lurch. 'And that
part of my life is closed. I know how dangerous
you are, David, how bitter and ruthless. It's all
there in your face. You've changed.'

'We all change when life is cruel to us.'

Absurdly, because nothing could assail her love
for him, she tried to offer comfort. 'I'm sorry,
David. I'm sorry.' Her voice broke on her last
words.

'Words, little one,' he said with a curious echo
of his old tenderness. 'Presented with a compassionate face and a tender voice. A madonna. And
behind the emerald eyes the sweet-tongued wild-
ness, the promise of passion to the exclusion of all
else. The days of my enthrallment are over. You
taught me never to trust a woman again.'

Elizabeth felt so defeated she didn't even look
up. At nineteen she had felt just as maimed, a
young girl who didn't even look up when a com-
manding, bejewelled rich woman had chastised her
bitterly, flinging words at her she would never
forget, the melodic voice vibrant with outrage,
bouncing inside her mind. . . . *You are never, ever,
again to come near my son.* . . . Nadia Courtland
had not merely been telling her, she had re-organ-
ised her life. . . . *You see, I have the total support of
your uncle and aunt.*

'Repenting, Elizabeth?' David asked, over her
head.

She nodded several times.

'I know you'll want to tell your fiancé all about it.'

'*Us?*' she queried.

'Wouldn't it be wise before somebody else tells him?'

'No one knows.'

'There are always the ones seeing evidence in backgrounds. Anyone contemplating coming close to my godfather had better front up right now.'

'Why didn't you?' asked Elizabeth.

'Oh, I'm too much the gentleman.' He held her two hands to her sides. 'Men need protection from girls like you, Elizabeth. Even your Gavin.'

'He loves me.'

'Splendid. Then he might take it well.'

She raised her eyes and her lips parted. 'You used never to be cruel.'

'I'm going to compensate for all that now,' he assured her.

'I—I'll go away.'

'Indeed. Do you think you could bear it? You're a beautiful girl and you play the piano extremely well, but it's not all that easy to find yourself a personable rich man, even if he *is* old enough to be your father.'

'I care deeply for Gavin.' She saw herself mirrored in his black eyes.

'Darling, you can sing his praises until the cows come home, but nothing could convince me you love him. I'm not a stranger, Elizabeth. I left my mark on you and you left me pretty raw. I know you backwards, your body and your devious little mind. You had a cruel childhood with that saintly bitch for an aunt, but now you're within easy reach of a life-style you only barely imagined. Why, if you even tried you could have poor old Bill as well.

But you don't want the shadow of a man, you're too passionate.'

'Was,' she said bleakly.

David laughed at that, a cruel mirth. 'With women like you around, what chance has a man got? I've heard of nothing but Elizabeth for weeks. Your Gavin is assured a high place in the empire on your talent alone. Given the old man is a genuine music lover.'

'So you knew I'd be here?' Pulsating with agitation, Elizabeth finally freed herself from his grasp.

'How else did you think I achieved such a degree of suavity? While you, Elizabeth, went through the night in a trance. I expected you to be very heavy-handed at the piano, but you quite surprised me and scalded my heart. Even to the Debussy. What a silken touch!'

'I never heard your name once. Not until we were introduced. You were the mystery guest.'

'Well, well, well. I must admit when the Old Man mentioned your name I felt as if I was being hit over the head with a battering ram, then something about his proposition appealed to my perverted sense of humour. Anyway, I wanted to meet your fiancé.'

'Don't hurt him, David,' she begged.

'I'm flattered you think I could. Does he delude himself that you love him?'

'I think you intend to break up my engagement,' she heard herself saying aloud.

'A bit Freudian, isn't it? He could be a father to you.' She turned away from him despairingly and he caught her hand. 'Are you really the way you are because you were denied a normal childhood?'

'I know if I stay here being tortured by you I

shall go mad,' she retorted.

'Hell, Elizabeth, that sounds terrible. Torture—' he savoured the word, pressing his thumb into the palm of her hand. 'I'm beginning to enjoy the sound of that.'

'Don't!' She brought herself to look at him, tall, very lean and hawkish, wholeheartedly disenchanted. 'If there's something I have to do, I'll do it. I'm good at that.'

'Bitch!' He suddenly lost his grip on his control, choking out the word. *'Witch!'* He brought his two hands up around her throat, and if she had visions of being strangled they seemed preferable to what happened.

David watched her lips move soundlessly, then as though tormented by their cushiony beauty he covered them fiercely with his own, a dark rush of blighted ecstasy from the too well remembered past.

Five long, pain-filled years might not have happened. Elizabeth melted, just melted, with a wild, abandoned air, pressing herself against his body, moaning brokenly the instant his assaulting mouth gave her air.

'God, the perfidy of it all!' He almost threw her away so she staggered. 'What *is* it, Elizabeth, some insatiable lust?' His black eyes were glittering jets, flaring furiously.

'Oh, David, for God's sake!' She knew she was crying.

'I want you, do you accept that? I hate and despise you, but that's beside the point. I want you as I never expect to want another woman in my life.'

Lights seemed to be dancing around his head,

and a sweat broke out on her forehead. 'I think I'm going to faint.'

'More drama?' His tone was contemptuous.

She slid down on to the thick, springy grass, curiously intent on what was happening inside her. She was going to faint. Was going to . . .

She never even heard the sharp, quick intake of his breath. 'Elizabeth, hell. . . .' David said it as though there were no difference between the two words. She was as beautiful as a painting, a disturbed dream, and she was undoubtedly unconscious.

When she opened her eyes again, Marion was saying to David in a worried voice: 'You don't think she's——'

Elizabeth's green eyes were wider now, the pupils dark and distended.

'My dear little friend,' Marion addressed herself to the girl directly, 'what's happening to you? Last night and now this morning? It's so fortunate David was on hand to help you.'

Elizabeth pushed her head back into David's chest. 'I'm all right.'

'I'd be obliged if you'd stay where you are for a few moments,' he said.

Marion looked red in the face and absolutely baffled, while beyond her Solomon and Sheba sat in the shadows with their ears pricked enquiringly. 'If you're on some strict diet, say so. Diets are bad for young girls.'

A shaft of sunlight was coming through the trees, rushing for her like an arrow. It passed lightly across her face, dwelling on her flawless skin, the thick golden skeins of hair that streamed over her shoulders. 'I'm okay, Marion.' Her voice sounded hollow, without substance. 'I just didn't sleep very well.'

'Let me get a car to take you back,' said Marion, her mind passing over all kinds of things that might make a girl faint. Everything to her maidenly mind pointed to pregnancy, and it was then she first discovered she didn't approve of Gavin as Elizabeth's husband at all.

'How do you feel, kiddo?'

David sounded so much like his old, vibrant self that Elizabeth stiffened. Once not a single day had passed that the joy didn't stream out of him to her. 'About ready to get up,' she said as quietly as a whisper.

'Let me help you.' He lifted her as easily as a spent child, so she had to twine her arms around his neck.

The collies got up and moved forward with increasing momentum, wagging their beautiful tails.

'Down, boys!' ordered Marion with something approaching authority. 'I don't know why I always say that when Sheba is a girl. Easier, I suppose.' Something about Elizabeth and David was delighting her eye, an overwhelming sense of rightness, like two perfectly matched thoroughbreds. 'There, I was afraid of that.' Solomon jumped up, wanting reassurance, joining the tableau.

'Lovely boy, lovely.' Elizabeth buried her hand in the thick fur.

'Are you two really strangers?' Marion asked, not even knowing why she asked it. 'Oh, I know that's ridiculous, but you seem to relate.'

'How's it going, Marion, your work?' David set Elizabeth down and turned to the older woman.

Marion blushed scarlet and gave an embarrassed

little moan. 'Still splashing paint on the canvas. Some falls on good ground.'

'You paint?' Elizabeth almost sighed aloud in gratitude.

'Yes.' Marion smiled hesitantly at one, then the other. 'David always asks because David was the one to encourage me. He understands that an old maid has to have something to keep her going.'

'What about a passionate love affair, a tiger shoot?'

'More like a game of cards.'

'Shuffle them, sweetie. Throw them over your shoulder,' David suggested, and put his arm around her. 'You're a nice woman, Marion—all good points, none bad. Don't get depressed because you're not every man's dream. That kind of woman only churns a man up.'

'Half their luck!' Marion smiled wryly, her short, trim body clad in an unbecoming flowered smock.

She was rich, Elizabeth thought. Marion was certainly rich, so what was the point of all these bargain basement dresses? She knew precisely how Marion *should* look, indeed with very little effort a transformation could be achieved, but Marion had settled very early in life into rejection. She saw it all; a beautiful mother with an air of bewilderment every time she looked at her probably skinny little child, Sir William contemptuous of any female creature except she be extraordinarily beautiful. She saw it all. It was simple. Marion had probably settled into oblivion at five.

'You're looking very much better,' Marion said to her. 'Surely, though, you should see about it?'

Elizabeth stroked the thick, silky hair of Sheba's ear while the beautiful creature rubbed her head back and forth against her. 'I was only tired.'

'And needing your breakfast,' Marion cried like a forgetful hostess. 'What say we have ours before anyone?'

But then as they arrived back at the house Gavin appeared, immaculate as ever, and stooped to kiss Elizabeth's cheek. 'I say, have you all been for a walk?'

'It's a miraculous morning!' said Marion with almost childlike brightness, her eye falling on Elizabeth as though waiting for Elizabeth to admit she had fainted.

Elizabeth said nothing and neither did David, and after the two men had exchanged a few rather brusque pleasantries, they all followed Marion into the breakfast room that gazed across to the man-made lake.

'Oh, there are the swans!' exclaimed Elizabeth, compelled to go to the window. 'Such supremely beautiful birds.'

'Elizabeth is a very serious nature-lover,' Gavin supplied. 'All the way down she told me all about the shrubs and the trees she's going to plant in our first garden.'

'And when is the happy day to be?' David's face was half in sunshine. He had walked to the huge plate glass window as though he too found the sailing swans seductive.

'That's for Elizabeth to say.' Appeal spread itself out on Gavin's heavy, handsome face. 'She'll make an ethereal bride.'

The smile on David's face looked more like a little snarl. 'A white wedding and all the trimmings?'

'Oh, I should say so,' Gavin agreed, quite unaware. 'All our friends are expecting a big turn-out and Sir William has already promised us Bellewood for the reception.'

Thick black lashes covered David's liquid eyes, but not before Elizabeth had seen the flash in them. It would be impossible to avoid friction. Impossible.

'Now, Elizabeth, you must eat up,' Marion advised, as though the rejection of a huge breakfast would destroy her. 'Young girls are starving themselves to death all the time.'

'For love,' David said blandly, and moved to the sideboard where a dozen silver-topped breakfast dishes lay. The unknown, to Elizabeth, cook had supplied enough to feed six armies when she was the hapless type who couldn't really eat a big breakfast.

'Now here we are,' Marion was saying vigorously, in every way a thwarted mother, 'juice, fruit, the continental type of thing if you like,' she waved a dismissive hand at the freshly baked croissants, 'eggs, bacon, sausages, tomato. . . .'

'Lovely!' Gavin supplied heartily. 'I've rarely seen such a beautiful morning spread.'

When they were almost finished, Elizabeth far more than she wanted so as not to offend Marion, Angela arrived, dressed impeccably and giving every impression that she fitted beautifully into the Langley castle.

'Morning, everyone,' she greeted them.

'What will *you* have, Angela?' Marion asked, looking as though she was about to jump up and serve.

'Only coffee, dear. God knows I can't eat breakfast.'

'Forever on a diet,' Gavin whispered.

'I am *not* on a diet.' Angela came back and sat down in the empty chair beside Gavin, looking faintly irritable. 'I can eat anything I like.'

'Sorry, darling,' Gavin said goodnaturedly. 'I didn't mean to bring embarrassment on you. You have a superb figure, as you know.'

If Angela had been mildly upset she was now highly pleased, looking across the table and addressing her next remark to David, who was studying them both with a highly interested eye. Despite this quiet poetic engagement it would have been apparent to a halfway blind man that this handsome brunette would have liked to fling her arms around Gavin's shoulders and kiss him when apparently the gentleman was unaware of it. It was all there in a gesture, a certain way of looking. A triangle. How quaint.

Afterwards, Sir William, who took a gargantuan breakfast in his room, organised another business meeting in the study, and so as to not thoroughly antagonise his guests suggested they all make it for golf in the afternoon.

'We shouldn't despair,' Ellie told Elizabeth quietly. 'We must take the day—whatever it is— and make the best of it. How anyone can enjoy golf is a perpetual mystery to me, but I have dedicated myself to my man. Whither he goes, I go.'

'I can't even swing a club,' Elizabeth admitted, considering drowning herself in the lake.

'Never mind, have a go.'

Despite everything, it was a thoroughly enjoyable afternoon after Sir William and David went ahead, Sir William with a rather testy expression on his face. Women were perfect idiots. It was absolutely true.

'I *will* make you a golfer,' Gavin promised Elizabeth, sickened by the rhythm and power of David's swing. 'I don't want to make an issue of it, but that Courtland's an arrogant devil, isn't he? I don't often find myself disliking someone, but I mean, he's too much. What's more, he knows something I don't.'

Tell him now, Elizabeth thought, staring in dismay at the little mound of turf she had chopped up.

'Honestly, if you deserted me,' Gavin told her, 'I'd cut my throat.'

What could she say after that? It was apparent Gavin's position was under siege, as was usually the case in big business, and though she hated the deception she felt incapable of telling him about David now. Gavin was the opposite of a violent man, in fact he was always sounding off about the uncivilised, nasty little upstarts he must deal with and employ, but he had never before been helplessly in love.

'Some blighters have too much, don't they?' he was still saying, like a needle stuck in a groove. 'I swear that's what this whole weekend is all about. The old devil wants me to know without actually saying it that I'm not the guy for the top job. Bloody Courtland is. Who said there isn't any class system in this country—there *is*. Just because I started life a pauper . . . well, not exactly a pauper, I did go to the right schools. . . .'

Elizabeth let him ramble on without actually hearing a word. It eased him to talk, and Langley's course (it must have cost Sir William a fortune) was a wonderful place to walk and keep the blood circulating, her courage up. Perhaps David only intended to torture her for a while, otherwise why hadn't he exposed her at breakfast? What a diversion that would have been. Angela's avid face, the condemnation, I-told-you-so.

In the distance they heard Sir William's bellow. Someone, something, had offended him in some way. Certainly not his godson. Everything David did, he did brilliantly. Except that he had taken a wife he did not love and suffered the consequences.

The weekend wore away. Ellie, Marion and Elizabeth were companionable; Angela was bored to distraction when she wasn't with the men, forever afraid Sir William was going to ask Elizabeth to play the piano, which he often did, seeing her obligatory presence as a futile waste of time. At these times, too, Gavin was wont to gaze steadily into his glass, so that it was inevitable that the two of them seemed to form a pair.

'Your fiancé is rather dim-witted, isn't he?' David remarked mockingly as he closed down the lid of the grand piano after the Sunday evening's performance. 'I mean, do you think he can actually learn to enjoy your splendid talent?'

Every time he looked at her Elizabeth felt her whole body glowing, nerves keyed up so the blood glittered brightly in her veins. 'It doesn't matter to me,' she said quietly, which was true.

'Exquisite lunacy,' he drawled elaborately. 'Then again, the Black Widow thinks he's fantastic.'

'I don't care about that either.'

'No, a mere nothing. After all, you're not in love with him.'

The music over, Gavin was smiling, complimenting Sir William on a very fine brandy.

'Come down and see the cellar,' the Old Man grunted. 'We won't be stumbling half blind in the dark.'

'Not like the other time,' Angela laughed, very svelte in khaki silk evening pants with a lamé top.

'David, are you coming?' Sir William stopped, his all-seeing blue eyes gazing straight at the motionless pair curiously poised like a photograph at the piano. 'Elizabeth?'

David smiled his infrequent, devastatingly charming smile. 'Go ahead, Bill. I was just going to ask Elizabeth to take a turn with me around the garden. The time's been all too short, and I'd like to know more about this highly talented young lady.'

'I would say so,' Sir William beamed on them, keeping his cigar in his mouth.

'Did you say something?' David raised a laconic eyebrow as he heard Elizabeth's muffled gasp.

'I'm not going with you,' she said, catching their reflections in a lovely gilded mirror poised above a Regency commode. There were masses of pink and white roses in the room extending their perfume like no other flower. She stood there, captive as ever, feeling his hand come out and grasp hers. Not gently, courteously, but with a blaze of decision.

She had to go with him, the moaning sound starting up within her. 'Are you warm enough?' surprisingly he turned to ask her, his handsome face coldly brilliant, merciless. The white dress she was wearing fell in soft chiffon folds to her feet, but it had a tiny slip top. 'I suppose if I let you go, you'd run away and hide?'

'Would it do me any good?' she asked ironically.

'I'd be delighted to come after you.' He gave her a mocking, predatory look, a bitter, derisive man. 'It's amazing, you know, Elizabeth, how you always look so virginal. Fantastic really, when you know.'

'If you're going to unmask me, David,' she said, visibly flushing, 'I'd be obliged if you'd do it and get it all over.'

'Who, me? Unmask you?' He took her arm and led her out under the brilliantly blossoming stars. 'I'll let you do it all yourself.'

The garden, even at night, was a paradise of earthly delights, yet the air was poisoned with bitterness and intrigue. They had always come violently together, but once it had been in love, ravenous to be together because the mystery of what had happened to them was too big to be contained.

Decades ago. Eons. Now their every word rubbed against raw wounds.

'Melanie was killed, did you know that?' he said in a voice so clipped it cut her profoundly. 'My mother too.'

'I'm sorry, David,' she said in a broken, exhausted fashion. 'Marion only told me.'

'You don't read the newspapers?'

Even then she had been in Germany, trying to contend with her uprooted life.

'I never knew.' Her eyes focused on a classical statue of a Roman goddess, a miracle of white marble that presided over the terraced gardens below.

'Naturally. It seems to be your plan to deny everything.'

'It must have been terrible for you.' She swayed a little so the lights from the house shimmered over her caressingly.

'A time to break down. A time to mourn the mother I adored, a young wife who after all never hurt anyone in her life.'

'No.'

Elizabeth remembered Melanie, small and dark and very, very pretty. Nadia Courtland had loved her, the daughter of her dearest childhood friend, laying her plans that Elizabeth had so shamefully spoiled. Nadia and Melanie had been certain of David. Indeed, before Elizabeth there had never even been any speculation. One day the young couple would marry, uniting two rich pastoral families, and as a wedding gift Nadia had planned to give them a baroque painting long cherished in her own family that would have brought a fortune on the international art market.

In those days Elizabeth had been intimidated by wealth, thrown into its charmed circle by accident. Melanie had been an admirable girl, well educated, gracious, secure and self-confident as only pampered rich girls could be. But Melanie had never been unkind, not even when she fully realised 'Aunt' Nadia's alarm. Melanie had never been ruthless when she had to be. After all, she had Nadia, possessed of all the devilish qualities when something threatened her son.

'She was heartbroken that she couldn't become pregnant,' David told her. 'She loved me even when I acted as if she never existed. Melanie. It was never any of her fault.'

His tone, though quiet, kept Elizabeth absolutely subdued. Melanie and David sleeping together, man and wife as it had been planned right from the start. Yet she and David had been fated to meet, a curse perhaps on both of them for daring to love so extravagantly.

A night bird flew from the trees, dipping so close to them Elizabeth gave a little startled cry and put up her hand. 'Oh, it's only a bird,' she whispered in relief.

'What did you expect, a shrieking ghost?'

'You think I've wronged you.' The communication was still between them, the deep rhythm and unrestricted flow.

'Considering you gave yourself to me for hours, swore over and over again you loved me, told me in every way you knew how, until finally there was nothing more to do but get married, I suppose I *did* believe you utterly. Stupid, wasn't it, when stupidity isn't my style. God knows what your plan was, or were you in the hire of the devil, some dark enchantment?'

Elizabeth lifted her head to the glittering sky. 'You hate me now.' It could hardly be otherwise.

'I simply want the unhappiness you caused to overtake you now. I never did get to thank you for your poisoned letter. I would have strangled you then.'

She felt such shock her legs went weak. 'I sent no letter. Nothing at all.' Her voice gained strength, vibrating with intensity.

'Bravo,' said David with a fierce admiration. 'You're good!'

'I'm telling you the truth.' It had been part of her promise to Nadia Courtland that she would never attempt to communicate with David again. In any case, she couldn't risk it. Even then her own

loving family would have been too vulnerable.
Ruth, near hysteria, pitiless yet pleading, Jill's
sallow face frightened with all kinds of panics
chasing across it, Uncle Edward so pinched he
looked prematurely old.

Ah, the irony, when it was she who had had to
save them. Another inexplicable cruelty dictated by
fate. No doubt some lives were set in a particular
mould, terrible from start to finish. 'Where was I
supposed to send this letter from?' she asked him.

'Who the hell cares?' he retorted, maddened by
female irrelevance. 'You didn't have to resort to
such stuff anyway.'

'It was mine?' The motion of her delicate, naked
shoulders was ineffably dejected and sad.

'*Darling*,' he said automatically, his voice heavy
with contempt. 'It was your writing, no one else's.
Remember I had a whole lot more letters for
comparison. Your writing is very distinctive, just
like your brain.'

It was too late now to try and vindicate herself,
even with Nadia gone. Too much tragedy had
entered his life, an agony of remorse. Nadia, even
from the grave, would still triumph. Probably she
had even paid someone to do the writing, brutal to
be kind to her beloved son. Nadia in control of the
family fortunes and her son's future. However de-
structively she had acted, she had really believed in
her own omnipotence. Elizabeth she had plainly
seen as an adventuress, a lorelei washed up by the
tide. The only thing to do had been to throw her
right back into the sea, because she had fallen in
love with a mortal, to drown.

They walked for long moments without speaking; what was there to say anyway that would do

any good? Great banks of azaleas lined the walk, a dazzling array by day, ghostly pale by night. It was a dark path, moving farther away from the house.

'I think I'd like to go back,' Elizabeth said quietly.

David glanced down at her glimmering profile. 'I've no intention of murdering you. Not even rape.'

'Of which you made full use in the old days.' It helped her a little to say it, though it was far from true.

Apparently he thought so too, because he gave a low laugh without any pleasure in it. 'No, darling, you were willing enough, surely.'

'You hold on to your memories too long,' she said dryly.

'Don't you?'

'No.'

'If you want to use that argument you shouldn't faint or go ghostly pale. Your skin always was a clear indication of your feelings. I remember how white it used to go.'

As they turned the curve in the path a little breeze sprang up that lifted her chiffon skirt like a bell flower, spraying spent azalea blossoms on them like confetti.

'Oh,' she said, her voice faintly joyous, shaking her flower-starred head. 'Where did that come from?'

'The wings of night.' David put out his hand and lifted away a white blossom that was nestling in the gilt coil of her hair. 'How much do you want to marry your fiancé?' he asked her.

'Very much.' She stood there, very still, trembling, longing to cry out she wanted the quiet, gentle things, the shield of security.

'Why should you be happy when I'm s⌐ desolate?'

'I've lived with grief too, David,' she reminded him.

'Tell me about it.' His down-bent face was as hard as a stone statue.

She said quietly, 'I loved you.'

'Shut up!' The steely hands came up and pressed down on her shoulders. 'I always knew I longed a thousand times more for you than you did for me, but I truly never dreamed a mortal girl could be so cruel. It was only a game.'

'No,' she protested.

'You wanted money. You had to have it to follow your brilliant career.'

'Of course I needed money,' she admitted. 'I had nothing, you know that. It was your family that started it all, anyway. I would never have become anything but for them. Your grandmother encouraged me.'

'And how you repaid her!'

'I only ran away,' she protested.

'You lie. You collected thousands! *Money*, the mightiest passion of all. What did *I* matter? Probably you were beginning to grow tired of me.'

'No one could have enjoyed life more than you, David,' she said sadly. On the very day she had gone away he had been out riding with Melanie.

'It was wonderful—then.' The dark, handsome face was remote, far away. 'Long may you suffer.'

'Don't *say* that!' His voice frightened her so much she grasped his arm. 'I never meant to hurt you, David. I'm truly not responsible for all your terrible crushing blows.'

'I suppose in a way you're not. Not as much as I am.' David glanced down at the hand she had placed on his arm. It had a pearl-like lustre against the black cloth of his sleeve, yet he resented it bitterly.

'David?' Tentatively she spoke his name, her fingers tightening.

'I understand you now, Elizabeth,' he said harshly.

It took them a few moments to become aware that footsteps were coming along the path, then Angela's rich contralto voice uplifted on the night air. 'Where the devil could they be?'

And Gavin's answering laugh. 'Don't be silly, Angie, there could be a hundred paths or more they might have taken. Such a wonderful night! The sky's swarming with stars.'

'Your fiancé,' David breathed, and passed a weary hand over his eyes. 'How did you set your trap for him?'

'Trap?' Elizabeth's voice sounded driven and exasperated, but as she went to sidestep him, he caught her body to him and half lifted, half dragged her right off the path.

She couldn't cry out. *Couldn't*. Her heart was thudding against her rib cage, his left arm was around her like a steel bar. Gavin and Angela were coming closer, Angela laughing, no doubt clutching Gavin's arm.

'Darling,' she said, 'don't feel so bad. I think the Old Man is only testing you.'

'Getting a bit darker, isn't it?' Gavin protested into the mocking dark.

'Not afraid, are you, pet? Many's the time we two walked the garden path.'

They were quite hidden in the deep shadow of the trees, shielded from sight by the height of the shrubs, even so Elizabeth sank back against him feeling somehow guilty and lost. It should have been comic, this game of hide and seek, only David's hands came up to cup her breasts, sweeping up over their tilted curves until she was frantic for escape.

'Don't, David, *don't*!' Her head fell back against him, desire leaping out of the welling confusion.

He didn't listen, his thumbs teasing the nipples that had already hardened into need. The night was alive, intimate, enveloping them, the tumults of the past confronting them again. Elizabeth tried to remember that Gavin and Angela were only a little distance away, that there was enormity in what she was allowing, but David had always had this wild, terrible hold on her.

'Why don't you scream?' he whispered to her a little savagely, the caressing touch cruel now on her bare skin.

She wanted to wail like a lost child, but she was even more desperate for his mouth, turning in his arms so tempestuously she could have torn the flimsy bodice of her dress.

'What is it you want?' He gathered her hard up against him, his voice so low it was no more than a warm breath on her cheek. 'Someone who can drive you wild? Past reason, past anything?'

With his strong arms still holding her Angela's voice fell on them like a cascade of icy water.

'Damn it all, Gavin, you're no fun at all! I tell you, that girl's making you positively dull.'

'You've got to learn, Angie, I love her.'

They were almost beside them, hidden by the towering shrubs.

'You know as well as I do, she doesn't love you.' Angela's voice was both wounded and angry. 'In fact, it's my opinion she'll do you harm. I mean, where *is* she? Going off with that David. There's something a bit curious about those two.'

'In what way?' Gavin had obviously come to a stop.

'Oh, I don't know,' said Angela with a bitter uncertainty. 'Well, for one thing, they give the impression that each disturbs the other.'

'I know that,' Gavin answered more happily. 'Elizabeth doesn't like the chap.'

'My friend,' Angela said shortly, 'you don't know women at all.'

'I know you, Angie,' Gavin said with affection.

'But you don't want me, do you? Not like you want that girl. Men your age have no sense at all.'

Ever sensitive to references to his age, Gavin apparently moved on, for Angela's high heels clattered as she ran after him. 'Oh, come on, honey, don't be an old bear!'

Gradually their voices faded, and Elizabeth struggled for release.

'Well, that turned out rather beautifully, didn't it?' David said mockingly. 'I do think you could be at least normally jealous of that Angela. She's known your fiancé rather well.'

Elizabeth was shaking in body and mind, suspended between the present and the past. Her breasts were tender, her flesh brushed with tormented desire. To be enmeshed with David again. Once the willing captive, but never again. Little caring now, she tore her dress, she sought the opening to the path, her breath coming raggedly.

'Careful,' he taunted her, holding back a laden branch. 'You don't want to arrive back at the house dishevelled.'

'Gavin trusts me,' she informed him.

'More fool he.'

CHAPTER FOUR

FOR more than a week after, though the gnawing anxiety was never far from her mind, Elizabeth's life went on in its orderly pattern. She continued to hold master classes at the Rubin-Renault Academy and because she had been an impecunious student herself, she gave a good deal of her private time freely to several young pianists hopeful of a scholarship to that renowned and expensive private school of music. Three had been referred to her by the Sisters of the Sacred Heart Convent, excellent teachers for the formative years, two others by colleagues who had noted the children's ability at recent examinations. One young girl, Jenny Neilson, reminded Elizabeth of herself. Jenny wasn't an orphan, both her parents were living, but in many ways they were the most unlikeable couple Elizabeth had encountered in her role as a teacher. Despite Jenny's very real ability, neither mother nor father showed any intelligent interest or pride in her accomplishment and were actively hostile to the idea of paying more for her lessons. The nuns were practically teaching her for nothing anyway. What money there was, was being reserved for their son. The boy was their pride, bright at school, good at sport. In another year, he would be ready to go on to university. Paying more money out on Jenny was unthinkable. She was destined, like every other girl, to become a receptionist or a typist like her mother had been.

Yet Jenny, with all her little idiosyncrasies ironed out, could be brilliant. She had a natural affinity with the keyboard and though she was only an undersized fourteen she had a wonderful control of dynamics. Elizabeth was determined to help Jenny all she could. The others too, but they didn't have Jenny's problems. Money might have been missing, rich relatives or friends, but they were all of them, right down to the last little sister or brother, on fire with pride for the talented member in the family. Jenny up until now, except for the nuns, had battled it alone.

Because it was just as easy for her, Elizabeth travelled to the beautiful old convent to give Jenny her weekly lesson. Lessons usually lasted thirty minutes, but Elizabeth invariably gave the girl an hour. If Jenny expected to gain admission to the Academy in the following year there was a lot of work to be done on a set programme, especially the Sonata. At the moment, Jenny's technique wasn't equal to what she wanted to do, and that was a lot. But she had heart, great heart, the music was deeply felt from within.

Mother Superior greeted her charmingly, a handsome, well-bred woman with serene blue eyes. 'Mrs Neilson is here, Elizabeth,' she told her, still with a smile but definitely a warning. 'She wants to talk to you about what we're hoping to achieve.'

'Thank you, Mother,' said Elizabeth, then responding to the older woman's look, leaned closer to hear what was intended for her alone.

'Gently, dear,' Mother Superior warned, 'for Jenny's sake we must be as patient and diplomatic as we can.'

When Elizabeth walked into the music room, Jenny's face turned instantly towards her, the desperate tears still oozing from her eyes.

'Mrs Neilson, Jenny,' Elizabeth gave them both her sweet, illuminating smile. 'Is something the matter?'

'I wanna talk to you about this scholarship,' Jenny's mother shrilled out. 'All this practising is driving us crazy and our Johnny can't do his lessons. I mean, when is it gunna stop?'

'I try to play softly, Miss Rainer,' Jenny confided, a plain little girl with a big gift.

'*Soft?*' Mrs Neilson's throat worked, but no further words came out.

'The examination is in November, Mrs Neilson,' Elizabeth explained quietly. 'Only a few more weeks. I know it's a sacrifice for the family . . .'

'Not a sacrifice, Miss Rainer,' the woman said tightly, 'it's hell! Johnny has to do his homework, he's so good at school, which his sister is *not*, and my husband expects to be able to watch a bit o' television. Is that too much to ask?'

'Of course not.' Elizabeth sat down beside Jenny on the long piano bench. 'I realise the difficulties.'

'Oh no, you don't.' Mrs Neilson leaned towards her, both urgent and fretful. 'Bill doesn't want any more of it. Night after night, morning after morning, Jenny flinging out notes like a madwoman. I wish the piano had never been given us. Bill's mother it was—always goin' on about a bit of culture. Played the piano herself until her fingers got too puffy with arthritis.'

The talent had to come from somewhere. 'Perhaps we could arrange for Jenny to do more of her practising here.' Elizabeth knew by now that the nuns would do anything to help Jenny.

'She'd still be bashin' away at home,' Mrs Neilson pointed out. 'We can't keep her away from it when every other kid is watchin' the television. I mean, it's not *normal*.'

'It's normal enough to try harder for an examination, Mrs Neilson,' Elizabeth said mildly, conscious of Jenny's quivering frame beside her.

'Well, I'm sorry, but it's gotta stop.'

'*Mum!*' Jenny cried.

'I'm sorry, Jenny,' Mrs Neilson looked flushed and upset, 'I'm not doing this on purpose. It's simply that the family is more important than you.'

'I'll never make it without practice.' Jenny moved her hand up and down agitatedly along her wet cheek.

'It can't be helped,' her mother said grimly. 'Johnny has to be considered, your father—lord knows none of you consider me.'

'Would you be agreeable to allowing Jenny to come to me for a few weeks?' Elizabeth asked in her gentle voice.

'*You?*' Mrs Neilson was patently astonished. 'Why ever would you do that?'

'I have great faith in Jenny, Mrs Neilson,' Elizabeth explained. 'So do the Sisters. With the necessary preparation she just could win a scholarship and the rewards could be great. I'm very highly paid, you know, and I started out just like Jenny—with financial help.'

Mrs Neilson blinked and looked down at her hands. 'You've taken me by surprise. Of course now that you mention it, gettin' highly paid an' all, Bill and me do appreciate what you're doin' for our Jen. I know you're important—Mother Superior was tellin' me how you give recitals an' all. But that's laughable when you think about Jen. She'll never be *that* good. I can't listen to her most of the time. I mean, the stuff she plays. It's really got no tune to it.'

'Would you like to discuss this with your husband, Mrs Neilson?' Elizabeth asked as soon as the woman took a breath. 'As I'm a fellow musician all the extra practice won't bother me. In any case, I have a sound-proofed room. I know how terribly tiresome and repetitious it can get.'

'We couldn't pay you,' Mrs Neilson eyed her warily. 'I mean, I could send along some groceries. She doesn't eat much anyway. It's Johnny that eats us out of house and home.'

'That's quite all right.' Elizabeth turned to smile at Jenny gently. 'If your parents say yes, Jenny, would you like to come?'

'That would be *wonderful*, Miss Rainer!' Jenny's grey eyes lit up. 'Are you sure I wouldn't be a terrible nuisance?'

'I'm not promising anything, mind,' Mrs Neilson couldn't control a flicker of jealousy.

'Of course not,' Elizabeth directed an understanding look at the woman, 'you must speak to your husband.'

With Mrs Neilson out of the way, the lesson proceeded. 'Do you think they'll agree, miss?' Jenny asked once.

'We can't think about that now, Jenny.' Elizabeth glanced at her watch, and motioned the girl up. 'I'll play the fugue through for you and I want you to listen very carefully. The subject—the melodic theme, as you know—is introduced by one of the parts, in this case, the treble, and taken up successively by the other parts. You should hear distinctly the repetition of the theme. Shut your eyes if you like, and commit it to memory.'

Jenny was a quick learner. With Elizabeth to demonstrate how it should be done, to emphasise the composer's intentions, the child was more easily able to utilise her own abilities. The next time she played the fugue through, it was with respect and understanding. Only after the lesson was over, for time was so valuable, did Elizabeth approach the subject again.

'It seems to me until your parents make up their minds, I'd better lend you my dummy keyboard. It comes in handy for practising in hotel rooms or anywhere where people don't want to be disturbed by the noise.'

'But I won't hear the music.'

'You will in your mind. You know, don't you, that Beethoven began to lose his hearing in his late twenties, but that didn't hinder his composing. For all his deep suffering and his loss of social life he produced some of his greatest works when his hearing was seriously impaired. Next week if we have time I'll play for you the first movement of his Appassionata Sonata. So you see, it *is* possible to hear the music in your head.'

'I gather you've wrought some miracle, from the ecstatic expression on Jenny's face,' Mother Superior said later when they were having a cup of tea together.

'If I have I expect it's due to your prayers.' Elizabeth looked at the older woman with faintly troubled green eyes. 'I suggested to Mrs Neilson that Jenny might come to me until the day of the exam. Apparently Jenny's practising has been driving them crazy. The only thing that bothers me now is that Jenny might be devastated if her father doesn't agree.'

'Poor Jenny,' Mother Superior sighed, 'so much superior ability, and yet in her parents' eyes she will never match up with her brother. *He* is their pride and joy—you have no idea! Anything he asks for he gets, to the exclusion of his sister. It's a terrible thing for a little girl to be confronted with rejection. God has been good in giving her her ability. She's beginning to act more normally. We had a lot of problems with Jenny at one time. She felt forced to be naughty to gain some attention.'

'She behaves perfectly with me,' said Elizabeth.

'You're making her very happy. To be able to play, play, play, that's Jenny's whole life. She's not at all good at school, unlike her brother. Actually John has quite a keen intellect. It's his manner that is quite woeful. His parents have spoiled him dreadfully.'

'From your knowledge of the family, Mother Superior,' Elizabeth asked, 'do you think Jenny will be able to come? Without a good deal of practice she's going to miss out. Positions are few and there are some brilliant young candidates. I have one at the moment that Jenny might find it exceedingly difficult to beat. Fortunately the boy has the most considerate and understanding of parents.'

Mother Superior set down her beautiful Aynsley teacup and stared out the window. 'I couldn't hope to forecast what the decision might be. It all depends on *Mr* Neilson's mood. I don't want to be uncharitable, but we have never had his co-operation. He's not a man who carefully weighs up the pros and the cons, he makes spur-of-the-moment decisions and sticks with them regardless. I just hope Mrs Neilson doesn't rush him—you know, tell him the moment he gets in. If he's had a bad day he could very well say no under pressure.'

'Oh dear!' Elizabeth felt an oppressive weight on her shoulders. 'Poor little Jenny. Perhaps I've done more harm than good.'

'Let's wait and see,' Mother Superior said calmly. 'Actually, Elizabeth, you've been extremely kind to Jenny, the work you do for other young people. Probably Mrs Neilson didn't even bother to thank you for giving so generously of your time, let alone without a fee.'

'She did, as it happened,' Elizabeth said, and smiled. 'She seems a most painfully harassed woman.'

'You don't know *Mr* Neilson,' Mother Superior repeated.

Elizabeth remained at home that evening to stay close to the phone, but instead of contacting her, Mrs Neilson put a call through to the convent. Mother Superior rang ten minutes later, an almost futile despair in her calm voice. The answer was— no. Mr Neilson didn't know Elizabeth and he didn't feel inclined to let his daughter go to her. Jenny would manage very well without extra piano lessons. He emphatically rejected the offer and to show what he thought of it scorned the customary thanks-all-the-same.

'Drat him!' Elizabeth put the phone down and flung a book at the wall. But she wasn't going to give up so easily. She would just have to try and see Mr Neilson—probably at work. Jenny had told her her father was a car salesman and Mother

Superior would know where. Not that Mother Superior had sounded hopeful—in fact she told Elizabeth she had just managed to keep her own temper. The bombast and the bluster had been faithfully reproduced in Mrs Neilson's stringy tone.

'Nothing can be the way *I* want it to be,' Elizabeth said aloud. The world was such a funny place. People were so odd. Didn't parents do everything they could to make their children happy? Playing the piano was Jenny's life, but if she ever became a pianist it would be without her parents' support.

The intercom buzzer sounded in the kitchen and, still feeling dejected, she picked up the phone.

'Elizabeth?' Angela Sutton's unmistakable tones filled her ear, causing Elizabeth a splinter of shock.

'What a surprise!' Elizabeth exclaimed, knowing she was in for further amazements.

'May I come up?'

'Of course,' said Elizabeth, somewhat nonplussed. The prospect of having a cosy chat with Angela was something to look forward to, but such were the social laws and regulations that she found herself opening the downstairs security door that protected her second floor apartment instead of telling Angela to go away.

'Nice place you have here,' Angela started out. 'And high too. A wonderful view.'

'Come in and sit down.' Elizabeth closed the door behind them and gestured Angela into the open plan living-dining room.

'Um, interesting,' Angela nodded her sleek dark head approvingly. 'Arty people tend to overdo things, but you've got everything quite nice.'

'May I offer you something?' Elizabeth asked.
'Sherry, coffee?'

'A whisky would do nicely. Over ice. I know you
must have some. A really good Scotch is Gavin's
favourite drink—and mine.' Very graciously she
sank into a cosy armchair, crossing her long
shapely legs and looking down at them approvingly
and from there to her beautiful Italian shoes. Very
self-satisfied was Angela, and she had reason to
be. Elizabeth had never seen her that she hadn't
been impeccably turned out.

'Chivas Regal do you?'

'Lovely.' Angela fixed her dark eyes on a pair of
cameo glass vases with silver mounts that adorned
a little side table. 'Where did you get those?' she
demanded sharply.

'Gavin.' Elizabeth had an impulse to match her
tone to Angela's. 'He bought them for me at an
antique auction. We often go around the shows
admiring, but I had no idea he intended to get those
for me. They were very, very expensive.'

'My dear girl, they look French.'

'They are—circa 1895, I think.' She set a crystal
tumbler down on the coffee table in front of
Angela, then sat opposite her, wondering what all
this was about. Angela had never taken it into her
head to visit her before. In fact Angela had never
cared when many of her unkind little remarks had
found their way to Elizabeth. She had even made
it easy telling the right people.

'*Wonderful!*' Angela took a mouthful of whisky,
rolled it around her tongue, then swallowed.
'You're not having any yourself?'

'I have a feeling I should have a clear head.'

'By their sins ye shall know them,' quoted Angela.

'I didn't think you were religious,' Elizabeth remarked.

'You look so innocent,' Angela drawled, sounding flattering and admiring. 'How do you *do* it?'

'It's easy enough when you are.'

'Naughty!' Angela smiled sharply. 'I've been having a wonderful time finding out about you.'

'Oh, yes?' Elizabeth lifted her delicate brows. 'Is this the reason for our get-together?'

'I knew there was some kind of link between you and David Courtland,' Angela explained. 'I'm very intuitive.'

'You mean you have a great craving for gossip.'

'Careful, dear,' Angela jeered. 'I could harm you.'

'In what way?' Now she was under attack, Elizabeth was quite calm. 'Do you think when Gavin knows he'll abandon me?'

'You don't love him!' The words burst out of Angela eruptively. 'All you're interested in is his money, the kind of life-style you're likely to have.'

'I'm sorry Gavin didn't fall in love with you, Angela,' Elizabeth said.

'He would have married me,' Angela declared vehemently, 'only you turned up to mess everything up. Gavin falls in love with you—temporarily. Who's to blame him? Even I can see you're beautiful, but that's all you have—beauty, and your wretched playing. Gavin doesn't care a fig for that. In fact, my dear girl, he finds it a terrible bore.'

'Otherwise,' said Elizabeth, 'he's a very nice person. We're very happy together.'

'You're only fond of him,' Angela said bitterly. 'How do you think he's going to feel when he finds out you're the most appalling liar?'

'I can't see I've merited that,' Elizabeth said mildly. 'I had planned to tell Gavin I knew David in my own good time.'

'He was your lover,' Angela accused her. 'Why, the way I heard it you two were crazy about each other until you got kicked out.'

'A long time ago.' There was no anger in Elizabeth's iridescent eyes, only a frozen calm.

'You don't deny he was your lover?' Angela cried.

'You'll believe what you want to.' Elizabeth stared back at the older woman's full, beating throat. 'Either way, Angela, virginity isn't the big deal it used to be. You and Gavin, for instance, were intimate, but *I* must understand.'

'I kept nothing from Gavin. *Nothing.*' Angela glared at her as though she were the most odious cheat. 'Though it seems you've kept from him a great deal. Why, the Courtlands financed your music studies from the age of fourteen. It was they who sent you to Sydney and later to London. And how did you repay them? With scandal, that's what. David Courtland was all but engaged to a beautiful girl, a perfect girl, he'd known all her life. But what did you do? In typical, vulgar, upstart fashion you set your cap at him.'

'*Set your cap!* What a dated expression,' retorted Elizabeth.

'What else have we? Seduced?'

'What business is it of yours, Angela?' Elizabeth was determined to maintain her calm, though Angela's expression was rather terrible.

'I'm safeguarding Gavin. I've been watching you constantly ever since you got engaged. You're an unscrupulous opportunist. The way you butter up

Sir William makes me feel sick!'

'Now there's something I couldn't do,' Elizabeth gave an ironic little smile.

'Oh, come now, he bought you that grand piano.'

'He replaced a very ancient Bechstein with a magnificent new instrument. He can afford it, and Marion plays.'

'Marion!' Angela exclaimed. 'Never mind poor old Marion. You're a very sly, slippery young lady indeed. You have Marion eating out of your hand.'

'Whereas *you* make the terrible mistake of thinking Marion stupid. She's not, far from it.'

'Marion is not worth discussing.' Angela's nostrils flared impatiently. 'Perhaps Gavin will begin to see you as you are—his golden girl loving someone else to desperation. And that's how it was, wasn't it? My sources were very well informed. You caused much tragedy and grief. The aunt you used to live with went on record as saying all you ever cared for was yourself. You didn't even write to them, you miserable, ungrateful creature.'

'If you've quite finished, Angela,' Elizabeth said pleasantly, 'why don't you clear out?'

'I'm going to damage you,' Angela said viciously, 'in any way I can.'

'You're going to tell of a supposed sexual relationship I had with David Courtland, is that it?'

'I'm going to tell a few interested people the truth about your background—the awful way you treated your family, the pain you caused the Courtlands. I know for a fact that your David has never forgiven you. He may have tried to be sociable at Langley, but I saw the spirit behind it. He hates you, and he has cause.'

'What's more,' Elizabeth said with forced light-
ness, 'you hate me too.' She stood up and looked
down at Angela still sitting like stone in the armchair. 'Do your worst, whatever it is.'

'On the other hand,' Angela suggested bitterly,
'you could be reasonable. Break off your engagement to Gavin and I give you my solemn promise
not to breathe a word.'

'Solemn promise? Could I trust you?' A grim
little smile played around Elizabeth's tender
mouth. 'You've done everything you could to
undermine me with Gavin ever since we met.'

'Because you're no good for him, that's why!'
Angela too leapt to her feet, the same height as
Elizabeth but very much more rounded and
mature. 'He's only your passport to the good life.
To go back to your childhood, you had nothing.
An orphan forced on relatives who could barely
afford to support you.'

'My uncle had a good job with Courtlands,'
Elizabeth said, her finely cut features tightening.
'My own parents left adequate money for a time.
We weren't really poor, I assure you. I was just
made to feel poor.'

'That's not what your——'

'Aunt said?' Elizabeth finished softly. 'Have you
entered into some kind of communication with my
aunt?'

'Apparently you have no family feeling,' Angela
evaded the question, finishing the whisky in one
belt. 'Let us get to the root of the matter. Break
off your engagement to Gavin and you'll hear no
more from me. That is my promise, and I'll give
you one week. Sir William too, you realise, would

have to be told. He thinks the world of you at the moment, poor silly man.'

'Sir William, *silly*? Imagine that!' Elizabeth walked to the door and held it open. 'Well done, Angela.'

'You're not fooling me.' Angela swept past her in a cloud of perfume. 'Under that cunning exterior is a frightened girl. If you want my advice, see if you can arrange an overseas tour. There's remarkably little for you here.'

Angela sailed out, dark eyes flashing, spoiling the effect somewhat by tottering on the stairs.

Some days, Elizabeth reflected bitterly, it hardly seemed worth the bother to struggle with fate. One could always count on people like Angela to deliver the knock-out blow. Yet despite Angela's visit one thing worried her more than all her mammoth qualms—what was going to happen to Jenny. She had the mystic feeling that if she could at least help Jenny, she could disappear without a trace.

By the following morning, because there wasn't time for delay, Elizabeth had decided on trying to see Mr Neilson at his work.

'Good luck!' Mother Superior had told her rather desperately. 'We're all praying for you.'

Mr Neilson was out with a client when she called and she had a forty-minute wait before he returned.

'Oh, hello there!' He strode into his office, a big florid man exuding affability. 'Come to get yourself a neat little car?'

'No, Mr Neilson,' she said, 'I've come to speak to you about Jenny. I'm Elizabeth Rainer.'

'Oh yes?' he said aggressively. 'I thought this thing was straightened out last night?'

It took two to make a quarrel and Elizabeth wasn't making one. 'I want to apologise to you for not coming to you directly in the first place. Of course you don't know me and you have every right to be protective of your daughter, but I do assure you I'll look after her well if you allow her to come to me.'

Outfaced by her direct glance, he turned away, taking off his jacket and flinging it over a chair. 'You must have precious little to fill in your time?'

'Actually,' she said evenly, 'I'm very busy and I know you are too, so I won't waste your time. I've explained to Mrs Neilson that Jenny is a very talented little girl.'

'I hadn't realised,' he said sarcastically. 'My son is my only solace.'

'You must be very proud of him,' Elizabeth said. 'Mother Superior at the convent told me he has a keen intellect.'

'Old bitch,' he said distinctly. 'A saint, to be sure, but she always looks at me as though I'm going to finish up in the hot place.' He picked up a nail file and began to use it. 'She's right about one thing, however, my boy's going to get somewhere. Not like me, a nothing. He's going to finish school, then he's going on to university—the first man in my family to do that. Education's everything these days!'

It was hardly the time to point out that many graduates couldn't find a job or that skilled tradesmen were becoming rarer. 'What course does he want to do?' Elizabeth asked sympathetically.

'Engineering.' Mr Neilson looked at her sharply to be perfectly sure she was sincere. 'He does seem to have a flair for mathematics and putting things together.'

'He's very fortunate in his father,' said Elizabeth. 'It must be a sacrifice for you.'

'Nothing too good for my boy,' the man said, a proud smile replacing the belligerence. 'If you only knew how furious he's been having to put up with Jenny's bashing the piano. First thing in the morning, before a man can hardly open his eyes, she's in full swing. Then again, when I get home, pounding away until I begin to wonder if the house is going to fall down.'

'It *is* annoying, I know.'

'Even the wife is distressed. Talk about silence is golden! I said it had to stop, with good reason. What would life be like with Jenny a pianist? It was my fool mother put it into her head. Teachin' her from when she was a baby, ravin' on about how musical the kid was. Never really noticed our Johnny, unlike most people. Everything about Jenny is second-best. She came second. She's plain and she's no good at her lessons. The top mark she can get is below average.'

'Well, she has one thing going for her, Mr Neilson,' Elizabeth said earnestly, 'she has it in her to make a very fine pianist, one who can earn good money.'

'Money, *yah*!' Mr Neilson made a vivid sound of disgust. 'What do you get, little lady?'

She told him, and watched him straighten up in shock. 'For playing the piano?' he asked dazedly.

'I had to work hard to get where I am,' Elizabeth told him, 'and I had to have help. My own family lacked the financial resources to help me, Mr Neilson, that's why this scholarship for Jenny is so important. It will pay all her fees and give her a small allowance.'

'And what if she doesn't make it?' He was back to his aggression. 'How is she going to behave then? I had to give her a good cuff in the ear this morning. That sobered her. I won't have a fourteen-year-old pushing past me, blaming me for everything.'

'I'm sure she'll come to realise you want the best possible thing for your children. It's not easy making all the decisions.'

'That's right.' For the first time he began to relax, a heavy man in his forties, alternating between brassy self-confidence and nervousness. It was easy to see he had a lot of complexes. 'What is it here you want me to do?'

Elizabeth's manner, always poised and self-possessed, became gentle. She leaned forward, fixing him with her luminous green eyes. 'To avoid causing all this tension I thought until the exam is over Jenny could live with me. I don't mind in the least, and—you'll appreciate this—I have a sound-proofed room.'

'Go on,' he chuckled. 'Of course you're a professional career woman.'

'Even if Jenny marries,' Elizabeth pointed out quickly, 'giving music lessons could bring her a nice little income.'

She couldn't have thought of anything better. 'Well,' he said consideringly, 'I'll have another talk to the wife and see what she thinks.'

'And you'll let me know?' Elizabeth stood up.

'Oh yes.' He picked up a pen and threw it across the desk. 'Thank you for coming.'

'I'm very glad I came.' At the door she turned to smile at him again. 'Whatever suits you, Mr Neilson. If you want Jenny at home at the weekend, I'll be pleased to drop her off and pick her up from school on Monday afternoon.'

'We'll see,' Mr Neilson said with a poker face. 'So long, little lady. I've a notion you could have made a place for yourself with the Diplomatic Service!'

CHAPTER FIVE

WHEN Gavin found out that Elizabeth was to have a child staying with her, his dismay was ludicrous.

'But, darling,' he held his beautifully manicured hand across his eyes, 'is this necessary?'

'I'm afraid so.' They were due at the private unveiling of Sir William's most recent portrait, but still Gavin stood there as though rooted to the spot.

'Hasn't the child got parents?'

'They're not very happy with a pianist in the family.'

Small wonder! Gavin thought guiltily, remembering great crescendos of scales. 'Why, it will be impossible for the two of us.'

'In what way?' She stood on tiptoe to kiss him. 'I mean, you haven't moved in yet.'

'You can't expect me to believe we can have a tête-à-tête with a child staring at us?'

'Nevertheless we shall have to cope. It's only for a few weeks anyway.'

'I won't. I won't share you!' he grumbled like a great child himself. 'Don't you get tired of doing these good works?'

'It's very little really. I'm just helping a little girl who needs help. I know you're going to like her.'

'I won't. I shall hate the little beast!' Gavin was plainly put out and added: 'I suppose she's got a moon face as well.'

'Come on now, stop feeling so irritated,' Elizabeth said firmly, 'you're so accustomed to having your own way.'

'Perhaps it's the only way I can live.' Gavin pulled at his black tie. 'Are you sure the real reason isn't to keep me out?'

'Oh, don't be so silly!' She picked up her evening bag and slipped it over her shoulder on its gold chain. 'How do I look?'

'Moving,' Gavin said valiantly, 'as beautiful as a lily, and you're going to be jostled and smoked over by too many people. I hate these damned cocktail parties. They're so inconvenient, and I hate standing up.'

'I'm afraid you're rather upset tonight,' Elizabeth observed. Gavin's face was pale under its habitual light golden tan. 'Anything I should know about?'

'I don't want to talk about it, darling. Not yet. Maybe later, when we come home.'

The cocktail party was held in the huge auditorium adjoining the Langley Board Room and by the time they found parking amid the Rolls, Jaguars, Daimlers, Mercedes, B.M.W.s and a few Porches it was almost the unveiling hour.

'Gosh, what a crush!' Gavin muttered unhappily, stiffening in resentment to see way across the room Sir William in conversation with the State Premier and several bigwigs, David Courtland by his side.

'Oh, persecution!' Elizabeth thought, knowing she would have a few unpleasant moments to face. David looked so comfortable, so perfectly right beside the Big Man, she felt quite resentful for Gavin's sake.

'There's Marion,' Gavin hissed. 'Poor mad soul!'

Marion, indeed, was coming towards them, in so dreadful an outfit Elizabeth wanted to shut her eyes so she didn't have to look. Sir William was undoubtedly a tyrant who delighted in putting his daughter down; on the other hand, Marion would have embarrassed a saint.

'Ah, there you are!' She took Gavin's arm and he like a hypocrite kissed her, beaming at Elizabeth. 'How lovely you look, Elizabeth! I love all that sequin work on your little jacket. It's perfect.'

'A lot of people here, Marion,' Elizabeth responded. If she hadn't spent so much time on 'all her good works' as Gavin called it, she would have been able to arrange for Marion to get her hair cut and styled. People often found Marion hilarious, but Elizabeth thought it sad and she was, though she didn't realise it, a relentless do-gooder.

'Wait until you see the portrait!' Marion leaned closer, rolling surprisingly expressive eyes. 'I'm just afraid Father will look at it with glazed eyes. I mean, it's he to a T.'

'What the devil does *that* mean?' Gavin asked Elizabeth when Marion had wafted off.

'Some portraits reflect all the good things, others don't.'

'I don't suppose it's that bad,' said Gavin. 'He's a handsome old devil.'

'And he's gesturing for us to join him,' Elizabeth pointed out.

By eight-thirty, when the cocktail party was officially over, Elizabeth was feeling so sufficiently frazzled she seriously contemplated allowing Gavin to make love to her. There had to be someone to take David's place.

But no, after all that lengthy talk, Sir William,

in brilliant good spirits (he had laughed uproariously at his portrait), decided on taking a dozen of
them out to dinner.

'Wasn't the artist naughty?' Ellie Whitney
confided to Elizabeth is private. 'He made him look
just like he is—an old devil.'

And he had to be, surely, because once again
Elizabeth found herself beside David at Sir
William's direction.

'I must say you're looking remarkably beautiful,'
David said with a pronounced undercurrent of
mockery.

'You're prejudiced, that's all,' Elizabeth retorted,
her cheeks quite flushed and her eyes like precious
gems.

But David had always turned the tables in the
most grievous way. Instead of looking angry or
hostile he laughed, his lean cheeks creasing in the
most attractive way. 'Please don't be upset, Elizabeth, if Bill's going to pair us off all the time. He
just loves extraordinary, complicated rela-
tionships.'

'*Does* he?' she said bitterly.

'For one thing, he's put your Gavin beside
Angela,' David said waspishly. 'There's no fun in
the world, is there, unless you can use people like
pawns.'

'And you've made such an impression on him
too!' Elizabeth was in the difficult position of
having to smile in the spotlight when she felt like
shrieking with jangled nerves.

'Probably because I don't try.' David too was
smiling, but his black eyes were hard and steely.
'This is supposed to be a celebration. Let's dance.'

She could scarcely sit there and battle it out.

Somehow she was on the dance floor where people were behaving erratically in the modern manner, many with no sense of rhythm at all but lively all the same.

'What is it you admire in your fiancé?' David asked.

On the crowded dance floor, she had enough cover to grit her teeth. 'He's a very clever man.'

'That hardly fits in with what I've seen of him.' Their bodies came together, never quite touching.

'Fortunately Sir William disagrees.'

'He's not the man to move into Sir William's shoes. Sorry, kiddo, were you counting on it?'

'I can leave you here,' she retaliated.

'I'm asking a serious question. Because if you were, you're due for an almighty shock. Your fiancé's a good man to have around. He's very capable, loyal, diplomatic and honest, it's simply that these qualities are the prerequisites of an offsider.'

'Are you telling me something?' she said sweetly, shivering as his hand touched her bare skin.

'Yes.' His black eyes scrutinised her flushed face. 'In front of this whole gathering, Bill is going to put me forward as his logical successor.'

'That doesn't mean you'll make it,' she said hotly, wanting to weep for Gavin.

'Darling, haven't you ever thought I too would become a living legend?'

'I want to sit down,' she said with the swift, absurd desire to cry. Indeed her eyes shimmered with tears.

'Don't you damned well do that,' he muttered. 'Damn you, Elizabeth!' He caught her to him now in the old, conventional style, his wide shoulders shielding her from curious eyes.

'I hate you,' she whispered, forever fighting a hopeless yearning. Being together was so intense, so intimate, she was frightened it might be showing on her face.

'Your body tells me differently, Elizabeth. Your eyes. It's something beyond us, that's all, something I can't put a name to. It's not love. I feel brutal.'

'Why is he being so cruel to Gavin?' She lifted her head, her heavy lashes spiky with blinked back tears.

'He's being himself, that's all. In your fiancé's place I would never have allowed myself such a golden, impossible daydream. That goes for the job, and you.'

'I'm going to talk to Gavin tonight,' she said urgently. 'I'm going to let him love me.'

'I've done that too, Elizabeth,' he said wearily, 'Desperation—it doesn't work.'

Towards the end of dinner, Sir William stood up and held up his hands, and David turned to glance at Elizabeth with a faint look of pity.

It was just as he had said. Looking strangely youthful for his years, Sir William Langley made it publicly known for the very first time ever that he had found the man he considered big enough to fill his shoes.

There was much reckless clapping, blazing jealousies, and Angela had a convulsive, coughing spasm that required Gavin to assist her from the table.

'There's another one who's desolate,' David murmured sardonically in Elizabeth's ear. 'I'm a rich man. I've been honoured, so why aren't I enjoying myself? Why aren't you?'

She heard his voice whispering to her all night. Once she turned over on her pillow and thought he was there. She could smell his male scent. It was still on her skin.

Gavin had come home with her, and Gavin, never a heavy drinker, had got drunk. He was now snoring—yes, *snoring* on her sofa that conveniently hid a bed. The first night ever he had stayed Gavin had flaked out, with Elizabeth tucking him up like a baby. It even occurred to her then, that a large part of her affection for him was maternal. In many ways, Gavin was a huge child, and he would probably require a lot of mothering.

'I can't do it!' she said aloud in piteous resignation. 'Angela is right. A good man might be hard to come by, but I know I have to stop this engagement.'

Her own face was flushed as if with a high fever. If only there was some antidote, some magic potion she could take to immunise her against David. But the gods were perverse. They liked playing with mere mortals.

In the morning Gavin was transfixed with a ferocious headache, but even then trying to apologise nicely.

'I'm so sorry, darling. I don't know what got into me. I was very upset.'

'Here, drink your coffee.' She put it down gently by his shaky hand. 'They say Vitamin C helps.'

'I'll be all right.' Gavin put his head in his hands, grimacing. 'God, I'll never get to work.'

'Why bother to go in?'

'Don't worry, I will. I'll wear dark glasses.'

While Elizabeth was dressing, the intercom

buzzer sounded and Gavin automatically answered
it, realising too late that a few people might not
possibly understand.

One of them was right below. 'Gavin? Angela's
voice bellowed.

'Good God!' Gavin enunciated so loudly, so
elaborately Elizabeth came through from the bedroom.

'Who *is* it!' No one ever buzzed her at that
hour.

'Angela,' Gavin retorted, saucer-eyed.

'I'm coming up.'

Across the room Elizabeth could still hear the
pealing warning.

'What on earth for?' Gavin asked very patiently.
'See here, Angela, what the devil's going on?'

'There are things that have to be said!' Angela
yelled harshly.

'Am I taking leave of my senses, or is Angela
shouting at us downstairs?' Gavin enquired, an
incongruous figure in a dress shirt and black evening trousers.

'Tell her to drop dead,' Elizabeth said tiredly.

'She must be drunk. Poor old Angie.' Clearly
Gavin wanted to help out.

'I think what she's trying to do, Gavin, is tell
you a remarkable story,' Elizabeth inhaled deeply.
'I have to be at the Academy at nine o'clock, so I
won't be able to stick around to hear it. Why don't
you invite her up?'

'I think we'll have to,' Gavin gave her a baffled
look. 'She'd be offended if we didn't.'

Angela, once merely jealous, was beside herself.
'You mean you *sleep* here, Gavin?' she shouted.

'For God's sake keep your voice down,' Gavin

pleaded, genuinely puzzled. 'Why are you so angry, and what are you doing here?'

'I rang you,' she said, gripping his wrist. 'You weren't at home. I rang last night and then again this morning. You *had* to be here.'

'Is something the matter? Is something troubling you,' he asked. After her late husband's tragic demise Angela had required a lot of counselling.

'Don't mind me, Angela,' Elizabeth said sweetly. 'This is only where I live.'

'She'll drop you now like a hot cake,' Angela predicted. 'I know her type. Something devious and dark is binding them together.'

'My head!' Gavin moaned, stricken. 'You're not making any sense at all, Angie, and I resent your lifting your voice in anger to Elizabeth. She's done nothing to warrant your abuse.'

'Ask her,' snapped Angela, her narrow dark eyes on fire like Medusa. 'Go ahead, *ask* her!'

'I daresay I'm still asleep and this is a nightmare,' Gavin muttered.

'You know, you've got an awful cheek, striding around like an avenging angel,' Elizabeth looked at the other woman with her own peculiar expression of disgust. 'What it's all got to do with you anyway, entirely escapes me.'

'I love Gavin,' Angela answered promptly, and Gavin immediately looked at her warningly.

'It's all right, I know.' As always, Elizabeth was merciful. 'I should think you could see, then, that he has a massive hangover.'

'Oh, Gavin,' Angela moaned in a strangled voice, 'I can't remember much about last night either. What he's done to you, the fiend!'

'I know it's probably silly of me,' Gavin

muttered, going very white, 'but you two are making me feel ill.'

'God forbid!' Angela wrapped her two arms around him and made him sit down. 'What you need is a nip of the dog that bit you.'

'What a beautiful domestic scene!' Elizabeth gave them both a look of amused horror. 'Personally, Gavin, I think you'd be much better off with Angela. I mean, I have a career and she could concentrate on you all the time.'

Later that very day, Gavin rang her and begged her to go out to dinner.

'Angela has told me everything,' he declared. 'Anyway, I don't care. Nothing is any fun without you. Angela is so bloody intense about everything anyway. Anyone can see you hate the fellow now.'

How nice it would be if it were only true. Her next pupil knocked on the door and Elizabeth had to put away any thoughts of her personal life. In fiction fiancés reacted differently, disengaging themselves quickly, immediately going out on the rebound with someone else to recover. Gavin *had* to be her true love because he simply didn't care what she did. It would have been wonderful had she loved him, but now others had begun to question her she was constantly forced to question herself. Had David not come back into her life, she would have gone ahead with her plans to marry Gavin and make him a good wife. Now she felt sorry for him and for herself. The only thing to do was drown herself in her music.

Jenny arrived at the Sacred Heart Convent with an Adidas bag stuffed to saturation with her 'things'.

'Has Mummy come with you?' Elizabeth asked. Surely mothers came to see their children off, have a word with the temporary guardian.

'No.' Jenny didn't seem to see her teacher's surprise. 'I really got the hang of the dummy keyboard. It's neat.'

The lesson started without any further ado, Jenny showing such progress Elizabeth decided just being a good teacher was enough reason for being.

'Excellent, dear,' she said in the cool, authoritative voice she used for teaching. 'If I have one criticism it's your trying to put too much into the third movement. Let it sparkle more, not sing. You're slowing the tempo up.'

'I'm beginning to believe in miracles,' Mother Superior said later. 'You must have handled Mr Neilson in the best possible way.'

Jenny had a wonderful time at the little dinner they had together, chattering incessantly in anticipation of the time she would return home and everything had to do with Johnny.

'Do you mind if I go and practise now?' she asked eagerly after they had rinsed everything and stacked it away in the dishwasher.

'Technique,' Elizabeth told her. But where another pupil might have lamented endless, dreary exercises, Jenny smiled, a touching little sight in her braces.

'At any rate Dad likes you,' she said. 'I heard him tell Mum you could charm the devil himself.'

'And bed at nine o'clock, young Jenny,' Elizabeth ordered. 'You don't want to drop in your tracks from over-practising.'

Jenny didn't reply. She was already through the sound-proofed door. The opening to a magic world. I just know she's going to make it, Elizabeth thought. The dedication at fourteen was formidable. All things being equal, determination would undoubtedly win the day.

Fourteen, she mused poignantly. At fourteen I'd fallen victim to a violent obsession. She stood looking at the cloudy light around a lamp, going back in time to the summer when she had first met David. It was a memory she had never consciously tried to preserve, it was just that their first meeting was burnt into her brain.

Of course he had never loved her. Not then. Intrigued, he said later. Enchanted, and not only with her playing. But then he was twenty-one, sophisticated and adult, an intensely brilliant young man with no small power over women. All the girls for miles around looked on him as a kind of god; his grandmother adored him, his mother looked on him as the most perfect achievement any mother could hope for. *David.*

It had not occurred to her that while she was playing somebody else had entered the room. There was only herself and the senior Mrs Courtland, that wonderfully distinguished old lady who had always remained her friend.

'Beautiful,' he said, and walked to the piano. '*Beautiful*. Shall we go for a walk and you can tell me all about yourself.'

And so they had walked into obsession, a kind of crisis that worsened every time she had come home on vacation. From the beginning she had written to him, and if he didn't write as often in the early days he had certainly replied.

'Fighting the madness!' he had told her. 'I mean, you were fifteen, sixteen, a child. A ravishing child but a child nevertheless.'

By the time she was eighteen it had become im-

possible to control their desires. The first time
Elizabeth had slipped away in a dead faint and
David had nearly gone crazy thinking he had
harmed her. The rapture had been too great, a
pinnacle of emotion that had made her cross over
into unconsciousness. She knew from the talk of
the other students at the Conservatoire that sex
could mean nothing. It had meant everything to
her: a meeting of bodies and minds and spirits. She
felt as though she were David and he were her.
Two bodies, one flesh. The joy had been chaotic,
though it wasn't at all simple to find excuses to
meet. He was David Courtland, with every passing
year a man to watch. She was the Courtlands' clever
little protégée. It would have been assuming far too
much to think she could ever meet them as a social
equal. The Courtlands lived exclusively in their own
world, families of high achievers with old money.

'You've taken on more than you can handle, my
girl,' Aunt Ruth had told her with unconcealed
malice. 'Jeopardise your uncle's job and we won't
want to see you again.'

The delicate wineglass fell out of her hand, landing harmlessly on the thick carpet. As if Uncle
Edward had needed her to do that! After thirty
years of conscientiously slaving for the Courtland
interests Uncle Edward in a moment of aberration
had broken all the rules and in doing so had played
directly into Nadia Courtland's hands.

'A common *thief*!' She had announced it like a
sentence, all the contempt in the world in her brilliant blue eyes. 'I wish to God I could call in the
police, get him arrested, but instead *you* must bear
the punishment exclusively. If you don't do as I
tell you before the morning is over, your contemp-

tible uncle will be in jail.'

So she had locked all she possessed in an old leather suitcase and gone about introducing a new element into her relationship with David, a feckless cruelty, a teasing and withdrawal that left him angry and baffled. A few days she had had to create a new image, excelling at it, no question of it, because if she hadn't, Nadia Courtland would take action.

After that, she just disappeared. It was easy when one could afford it and it had been imperative that she take the money. There were to be no misunderstandings. She had to obey all Nadia Courtland's dictates to the letter. Unequivocal surrender. At seven an orphan, at nineteen an exile. It must have occurred to Nadia Courtland that notwithstanding her inexplicable behaviour, David would try to follow her. The letter he had referred to, the letter he had never bothered to have verified, must have made him recoil in revulsion. Heaping sins upon her head. She supposed she could spend the rest of her days denying it, but David would never accept the kind of woman his mother was. After all, never in his life had he seen her ruthless side, only her pride and her worship. If it came right down to it Elizabeth herself could never attack his mother. Not now. One could not utter a word against the dead. She and David, enemies—that was how Nadia Courtland had wanted it.

A few feet away, behind the padded, sound-proofed door, Jenny was pouring her heart out on Tausig.

'Get out there and win, Jenny,' Elizabeth whispered. 'Winning is everything.'

Only it had never been for her. Everything was David.

As things would have it, Elizabeth found it very difficult to usurp her little lodger at the piano. Once she had to physically lift Jenny away from the keyboard, explaining that she had a concert the following Saturday night, a guest appearance with the Symphony Orchestra playing the ever popular Rachmaninoff Second Piano Concerto.

'Do you think I'll ever be able to play a concerto?' Jenny asked, her small face alight with heroine-worship.

'Not only play it, conduct it if you like. Now sit still and let me have a go.'

'Serves you right!' Gavin said wrathfully. He had not taken to Jenny in the least and Jenny, although she was too polite to say so, had not taken to him. Gavin, though he was a kindly man, lacked a way with children. In fact Elizabeth could well see he might find them disagreeable.

'I've been too long a bachelor,' he told her. 'Anyway, it will be different with us.'

Angela had tried her best shot, but the whole thing had misfired. Gavin was showing he really loved her, moreover, his own slate was not unmarked. So she and David Courtland had been lovers? That was in the past. He, Gavin, was her fiancé now, so that settled the matter. 'Trust Angie to stir things up!' he commented.

To her everlasting credit, Angela did not tell Sir William. He knew. His spies were everywhere, an intelligence service second only to the K.G.B. When Gavin told her Elizabeth turned to him incredulously, but Gavin met her gaze with 'a whatever did you expect?' David Courtland was his godson. When he was dead it would be David Courtland who would take over a great organisation. The thing to do now was try to make a friend of the man.

'I shouldn't be surprised if he didn't want to patch things up as well,' said Gavin, thereby betraying, though his own feelings were very genuine, that they didn't run deep.

On the Saturday night she had to get to the concert hall herself, because Gavin had come down with a virus.

'Nothing to worry about,' he said. 'At any rate, not yet.' Gavin took his viruses very seriously.

For the performance she dressed up, bearing in mind what her old Professor had told her—always look the part. To hide the mechanics of pedalling she always wore a long, billowing skirt, in this case a peacock green silk taffeta very much in the romantic style. Fit the dress to the music, and afterwards the audience, mostly young people, went wild. Sound wasn't just part of their lives. One had to almost sell the product and Hugo Cowley, the conductor, whispered mockingly to her: 'I don't know if they're going crazy about us or the dress!'

Either way it was a bravura performance and she was modestly pleased with herself.

It was at the exact moment she bent down to receive an enormous sheaf of carnations and roses that she saw David. He was looking very handsome and sombre, so utterly out of the general run of faces he would have been conspicuous in a crowd of celebrities. Obviously he hadn't meant her to see him, for he was sitting off to one side, behind a girl with a hairstyle so tousled and bouffant she might just as well have been wearing a lampshade.

In an instant, from elation, Elizabeth felt like weeping. Within seconds, her heart beating so fast it seemed it wanted to burst free from her body. Fly down to where it belonged.

Damn you, David, she thought. Oh, damn you . . . damn, damn, damn . . . whatever my sins, and she couldn't think of one immediately, I've paid, paid, paid. A strange kind of vertigo attacked her and she thought she might topple from the stage. More flowers arrived, and that saved her. Hugo came to her side.

'My, we *are* popular!' Hugo said happily. 'I really enjoy these youth concerts. The enthusiasm is wonderful.'

Quite a few of her colleagues and students managed to get around backstage to congratulate her, and after the last one was gone, lying in wait, was—David.

'Oh, hello!' The ordinary words trembled on her lips and behind them blasted love.

'You were magnificent, Elizabeth,' he said to her, his own mouth twisted. 'If there's nothing else that remains I find your playing unbearably beautiful.'

'I'm glad, David,' she said simply, her skin petal-pale.

'Don't you want a lift home?'

Briefly she considered telling him Gavin was calling for her, or she had her own car parked nearby, but intuitively she recognised that he had asked her because he knew she had arrived in a limousine Hugo had sent for her.

'I think it's all arranged,' she told him.

'We can manage on our own.' He brought his

black eyes to focus on her, not trying to dominate but doing it all the same.

'Really. . . .' she began.

'I want to talk to you.'

Her breath fluttered raggedly. 'I'll have to tell Hugo.'

'Then tell him.'

'He's in his dressing room.' She was suspended between longing and dread.

'Either you tell him or I will.'

Hugo assured her again how beautifully she had played and suggested they might do the Khatchaturian Carnival Week in a month's time.

The flowers filled the back of David's car, the combined scents startlingly heavy, the two of them locked in the shadowed interior of the Aston Martin. He didn't even say to her, where to? David never had nor ever would leave anything to chance.

They never spoke a word all the way to Elizabeth's apartment. There was no question of small talk between them. David's driving was in complete contrast to Gavin's—quiet, confident and fantastically silky. Gavin always seemed to have battles from beginning to end—fools who got in his way, frustrations with unclear signals, some minute little thing not working properly on his beautiful car, idiots who tried to challenge him. Only on the open road where nothing could get in front of him was Gavin able to settle back and relax.

At her door Elizabeth turned her face up to him, her graceful arms full of flowers. 'There's no sense in this, David, your coming in.'

'I'm sure there isn't,' he parried, and turned the lock. 'Go in, Elizabeth. These flowers need water.'

She didn't even attempt to argue but led him

through the apartment to the galley-type kitchen.
'I'll just stand them in the sink and arrange them
all afterwards.'

'As you like.' His tall, dark form moved back
and only then was she able to lift her hand and
find the strength to apply pressure to the tap. It
was the queerest sensation to feel helpless in another human being's presence, overcome by a sens-
uousness so powerful it required a tremendous
effort of mind to resist.

'Would you like something to drink?' she asked,
her mind leaping beyond the customary banalities.

'Tell me what Hartley has.'

'Oh, Scotch.' She grasped at some stems and a
rose thorn pierced the cellophane and entered her
thumb. 'Ouch!' she gave a little involuntary cry, as
beads of blood welled.

'Watch your dress.' Surprisingly David sounded
concerned, and because she stood gazing hurtfully,
he gripped her wrist and held her hand under the
cold running tap. 'Don't you know anything too
perfect is dangerous?' He glanced into her lovely
face. 'Where's some antiseptic?'

If only she could break out of this terrible languor. 'It'll be all right.'

'In fact pricks from rose thorns can cause a
lot of trouble. Don't you care about your hands,
Elizabeth?'

'Not really,' she exclaimed, which was perfectly
true. She even had to be organised into getting her
hands insured.

'Okay, so I'll find the antiseptic.'

'It's in the bathroom cabinet,' she said, too
genuinely entranced to move.

David came back within moments, drying her

hand and applying a little antiseptic cream. 'That really was deep,' he frowned.

'And the only thorn, I think,' she gave an emotional little laugh.

'It really needs this Band Aid. I'd better put it on.'

Now she was starting to feel feverish and the colour came up under her skin. 'Thank you, David,' she said tightly, and as quickly as possible pulled her hand away.

'Don't let it scare you,' he said. 'The electricity. We know all about it, don't we? Once we made the mistake of equating it with love and happiness, a delirious happy-ever-after. We're not going to be happy, Elizabeth. Either of us.'

She stared at him for a moment, then brushed by him, all her nerves shrilling. The telephone rang and she almost sprang to it. Gavin's attractive, faintly plummy voice sounded in her ear.

'I just wanted to tell you I listened to you on the radio.'

'And how are you feeling now?'

He let out a sigh that deepened into a groan. 'Dreadful! Don't come near me, darling, I beg you. My next-door neighbour has been wonderful, brought in some soup. . . .'

It seemed detestable, but David came to stand near her, frankly listening in. She swung around fiercely, her bare shoulders and her back taut.

' 'Night, darling,' Gavin was saying, deeply, desperately. '*Do* set our wedding date.'

'Why don't you put the poor devil out of his misery?' David said arrogantly.

'Actually he knows the truth.'

The handsome face was animated by a bitter

smile. 'He must be the only one who does.'

'Angela told him everything,' Elizabeth said.

'Angela?' His mouth quirked. 'Standing in the wings to take your place. Actually, she'll suit him a lot better. He's too old for you, Elizabeth, and much, much too staid.'

'While you are the most dangerous man alive. Dangerous to *me*.'

'I'm surprised you've finally accepted it.' The alien light flashed in his eyes. 'I will have that drink now. A good brandy if you've got it.'

Elizabeth crossed to a Chinese lacquered cabinet and opened it up. 'Who's looking after Ravenswood?' she asked.

'Ty.' David named his cousin. 'I don't want to go home again. I sold off a lot of the property to Uncle George and the two boys. It will remain in the family and I'm grateful they love it and will continue my father's work. I'm not a man of the land, Ty and Nigel are. It will suit me to take over from Bill when the time comes. He should have quite a few more spectacular years. He's in excellent health.'

She came back and stood before him. 'So it's settled, then?' Her green eyes were abnormally large and brilliant.

'Wish me well, Elizabeth,' he said with hard cynicism.

'I've always done that.'

'Sit down,' he said harshly.

It was an order and she threw her shining head back. 'You're altogether too arrogant, David.'

'You'd better get used to it.'

Spots of colour stained her cheekbones, a wild-rose flush. 'I'm going to do everything in my power to avoid you, David. It might be extremely difficult. . . .'

'Impossible,' he said dryly, and took a mouthful of the fine cognac.

'Do you really want me to break my engagement? What good would it do? It seems a miserable enough vengeance.'

'Miserable?' One winged black eyebrow shot up. 'To be forcibly parted from the man you love?' His jet black eyes flashed and the line of his jaw hardened. 'God, the men you exploit through your beauty! Doesn't the fool know you don't love him?'

'Did *you* know?' she flung at him recklessly, desperate to wound as she was being wounded herself.

She felt no surprise when in one movement he had her down beside him on the sofa, her body bent back so her head rested against the arm. 'It might help if you realised I won't be goaded any more.'

'Then what do you want?' She knew what he wanted with a certainty—a lifetime of torture.

'That's it, Elizabeth,' he said, reading her eyes.

'You could never force such a thing.'

'Who's forcing?' He put his hand under her chin and held it there. 'Whatever we felt, Elizabeth, it got warped and twisted, but the excitement is still there. You're as beautiful and destructive as you ever were, only this time I know what I'm in for.'

'*No*, David!' she protested.

'Can't you see the terrible rightness of it all? If you hadn't followed your path of glory, if you hadn't shown yourself a heartless little adventuress, perhaps two people would be still living.'

'No!' She tried to turn her head, but his fingers

were locked around her jaw.

'I thought I'd lost everything when you left,' David went on. 'Up until then our love had been a miracle. I had a whole world to conquer, no heights too impossible for you. I thought you the most remarkable girl in the world. Your beauty for one thing, your gift, the way you seemed so tender and compassionate, the things you liked and the things that made you laugh. I was oblivious to everything that was underhand and deceitful in you, the cruel streak. My mother warned me, and your aunt. Mean, truculent creature that she was, she still thought to warn me about you.'

'You *knew* me,' Elizabeth said tonelessly, 'yet you believed a woman who never spared me a kind word.'

'You tear at my heart-strings,' he assured her. 'If you ever decide to give up the concert platform you'll be able to exchange it for the stage.'

'Ah well,' she shut her eyes, 'revile me all you like.'

'Are you going to take your dress off, or shall I?'

'I won't help you, David. Not ever.'

'Oh, you poor, poor girl!'

Her blood surged even before he strained her to him and though she arched herself backwards he found her mouth, open on a little moan, the passion so ecstatic she was rigid no longer but moving towards him, his rapturous familiarity—David; there was no one like him.

He crushed the mouth under his, then began to explore it very delicately, breathing in his own name.

'David,' she was sliding into a feverish, drowning

state. Why should one man move her unendurably? *Why?*

'I want you,' he muttered.

She didn't protest when his hand sought her breast, moving her dress away from her, long expert. Then when she was scarcely breathing and half naked in his arms he began to make love to her, not with the tumultuous passion of the old days when it had been a wonder to come together and he had been as helpless as she, now he was nearly allowing her to scream with frustration, her head ringing with her own incoherent cries.

It was ravishment without release, a mind-bending, flesh-throbbing punishment.

'Seduction,' said David harshly, 'only this time the victory is in my hands.' He shook her warm, yielding body off and stood up as though violently beset. 'By Christmas time, Elizabeth, you and I are going to be married and there is nothing, nothing you are going to be able to do about it.'

CHAPTER SIX

BREAKING with Gavin proved even more difficult and heartrending than Elizabeth anticipated.

'Do you mean it was all true?' he demanded.

They were having a quiet dinner in a little restaurant Gavin favoured, and across the immaculate pink linen tablecloth he was groping for her hand.

'I wish I didn't have to hurt you, Gavin,' she said with tears in her eyes. 'You're very special to me.'

'But you don't love me?'

'I do!' She shook her head as though she was bewildered by her own actions. 'But not in the way you deserve. You're a good man, a nice man. . . .'

'Obviously Courtland is not.'

'I can't explain David,' she said. 'I can't explain what I feel for him or he for me. It's like a compulsive thing, an obsession.'

'Darling, you're not making sense.'

She stared at him with drowning emerald eyes. 'Maybe I fell in love too early and it stuck. David captured my heart when I was only a very young girl. Now I seem to be permanently in prison. There's no life with him, none without him.'

'You could have had a good life with me. You still can.' Gavin pressed her hand urgently. 'Is he frightening you in some way?'

'If one can be frightened of one's shadow,' she gave an odd little laugh.

'I ll kill him if he hurts you,' Gavin said violently. 'Do you really mean it, darling, what you say?'

'Please, Gavin. I can't continue our engagement.'

Her distress was so obvious he found himself patting her hand. He saw too that she did love him in her own special way, but it was only a faint glow to that other sorry radiance.

'Elizabeth,' he said sadly. *'Elizabeth.'*

She caught at the beautiful solitaire diamond on her finger.

'No, no,' he warded her off. 'I gave that to you, that's yours. If you like, I'll get you a matched diamond and you can have them made into earrings.'

'Oh God, Gavin, don't add to it!' Elizabeth felt like weeping hysterically.

'If it helps, darling,' he said quietly, 'I'm your friend. Always your good friend. Didn't I know down deep in my heart I could never have you for my wife? Well, so be it, but you've still got a friend. Now smile at me, precious girl.'

'Today a smile eludes me.'

'I think you're deeply unhappy,' Gavin frowned. 'I'm going to have a talk to this Courtland.'

'Don't, Gavin,' she warned him. 'Nothing has been easy for David.'

'He scares me a bit,' Gavin told her. 'I'm sure such a young man shouldn't have such distinct power. I mean, it's almost imperious and he's only new to the part. A few weeks ago the idea of his taking over from Sir William was greeted with raised eyebrows, now they're all at his beck and call, beaming on him, calling him the man of tomorrow. Mind you, he's brilliant without being predatory—a redeeming feature in my eyes. A strange man is Courtland. I expected to be shunted out, instead he's let me take over one of my pet schemes. Even the Old Boy couldn't see what I was getting at, but Courtland saw it right away. I suppose I'll finish up saluting him like all the rest, but never, if he hurts my girl.'

'*Aha!*' a voice boomed melodically from behind them, a voice they both knew.

'God, Angie, don't you ever give up?' Gavin demanded, his handsome face going quite pink.

'Forgive me, it's only coincidence,' she said. Coming behind her was a heavily built executive type.

Gavin rose to his feet for introductions while Angela darted many curious looks back and forth. 'Listen, why don't you join us?' she invited.

'Another time, my dear,' Gavin said smoothly. 'I have to get Elizabeth home early. She has a young student staying with her.'

'Is that a fact?' Angela laughed uproariously, while her companion stared blankly. 'We'll see you both later.'

'Poor old Angie!' said Gavin, permanently stuck in the groove.

Elizabeth was home before ten o'clock and Sally Forrester, her near neighbour, let her in.

'Jenny's in bed and fast asleep,' she told her.

'Thanks, Sally, you're a pal.'

'You've done plenty for me.' Sally insisted firmly. 'I've just made some coffee. Have a cup?'

'I'd be glad to.' Elizabeth was still recovering from her rush of emotion.

'What's up?' Sally asked sympathetically, 'and don't tell me nothing.'

'I've broken off my engagement, that's what.'

'Gosh!' Sally said wryly. 'We were all wondering if you'd ever get around to marrying him. I mean, he was a lovely bloke, Liz, but too old and too sober. A girl like you could get any man she wanted.'

'Not quite.' Elizabeth's throat tightened painfully.

Sally decided to change the subject. 'I let Jenny stay up to hear you on the radio. We both thought you were great.'

'Thanks, Sally.'

'Sit down and I'll pour.'

Elizabeth slumped down dejectedly and Sally yawned noisily. Even so, both of them sat there talking for well over an hour.

'Don't worry, Liz,' Sally patted her arm soothingly. 'Someone else will turn up. Mr Right.'

Mr Right, Elizabeth thought as she slowly prepared for bed. From time to time the tears filled her eyes, pity for Gavin, grief for herself. 'What's the matter with me?' she cried aloud, her head flung back to stare up at the stars. David couldn't force her to marry him. He couldn't drug her and push her to the altar. He couldn't make her do anything she didn't want to. He despised her. So why was she acting like a puppet?

I love him.

She whispered a prayer to the stars, but the stars took no notice.

The next time David came to her apartment, Jenny let him in, staring in some awe at the handsomest man she had ever seen. David inclined his head courteously, still considerably surprised to see her.

'And who are you?' he asked.

'I'm Jenny.'

'Where do you live, Jenny?'

At this point, Elizabeth came into the room. She was wearing a white robe tightly cinched around the waist and it was obvious she had just washed her hair, for it hung down her back in a thick golden rope, secured at the nape with a green ribbon.

'Hello, David,' she said, very cool and remote. 'Jenny is one of my students.'

'Live-in?' he gave Jenny a smile that made her instantly his slave.

'For a little while,' Jenny answered, her smile widening. 'Until the exam.'

'And when is that?' He took her hand and they both sat down.

'November the thirteenth. I just hope it's not a Friday.'

'It's not, Jenny,' Elizabeth, who had checked, told the child. 'It's a Monday, and your exam time is ten o'clock.'

'You mean you're a pianist?' David asked.

'Not like Miss Rainer.' Jenny blushed and cleared her throat. 'She's really wonderful, and she's awfully kind to me.'

'Naturally,' said David, 'she's an angel.'

'My dad thinks I'm an imbecile.'

'Oh?' David glanced away from Elizabeth and back at the child. 'Why do you say that?'

'Because *he* keeps saying it. He told me if I didn't stop practising, they'd all go crazy. That's why I'm staying with Miss Rainer.'

'Then I'm very sure you're good, Jenny.'

'Sometimes I am,' she confided. 'But I don't

think I'll be good enough to win.'

'What about the competition?' David looked up at Elizabeth who was still standing by the fireplace.

'Stiff,' she said truthfully. 'But at her best, Jenny just could secure a place.'

'At the Academy?'

'Yes.' She smiled encouragingly into Jenny's big grey eyes, the best feature in an otherwise homely little face. 'Which brings us to your practice time, Jenny. I want you to concentrate on the Prelude tonight.'

'Would Mr . . .?' Jenny looked hesitantly from Elizabeth to David.

'I beg your pardon, Jenny,' Elizabeth said apologetically. 'I'm forgetting. This is Mr Courtland.'

'*Enchanté, mademoiselle.*' David sprang to his feet and with considerable panache took Jenny's blunt-fingered small hand and raised it to barely brush his mouth. 'May I 'ave ze pleasure of 'earing you later?'

'Oh yes, please!' Jenny didn't giggle, but responded earnestly. 'I do have a party piece.'

'Wonderful!'

Jenny went off on Cloud Nine and Elizabeth waited for David to tell her why he had called so unexpectedly.

'Nice little kid,' he commented.

'She has a great deal of promise. She even reminds me of myself.'

'*You*, Elizabeth?' He raised an incredulous eyebrow. 'At Jenny's age you were a knockout.'

'I mean with the difficulties she's facing.'

'And what are they? Tell me, I'm interested.'

Of course he was. David had always been inter-

ested in everything; he was so vital, so alive. When
he was speaking to Jenny she caught flashes of the
David he had been—the unshadowed brilliance
and élan. There had always been laughter with
David, life was such a high-flung adventure un-
sullied by bitterness and remorse.

'What are you thinking?' he asked, his black eyes
totally absorbed in her.

'The way we used to be, the laughter we used to
share. You were the only laughter in my life.'

'What lies!' he made a disgusted sound. 'Sit
down, Elizabeth. There's really no need to stay so
far away from me. I have no intention of touching
you until after we're married.'

'Why then?'

'You know the answer to that one.' He watched
her move gracefully to a chair. 'Uncontrollable
impulses. Feeling that survives when everything
else has gone. It's not a question of love, Elizabeth,
it's more a question of compulsion. We're tied to
one another, to our grief.'

'And that's that!' She sighed deeply, unaware
that she looked, in her simple white robe, like a
blossoming lily. The light was caught in her lustrous hair so it glittered with every shade of gold
and even copper-pink and silver.

'Aren't you beautiful?' David said languidly,
raking her with his bitter eyes. 'And immensely
innocent.'

'I am.' In fact she was innocent of everything
except loving him.

'Not likely!' His shapely mouth twisted sardonically. 'Actually he's quite an appealing chap,
your ex-fiancé. I shouldn't be surprised if we finish
up friends.'

'Don't mock Gavin,' she said sharply.

'My dear Elizabeth, I'm not. I'm simply pointing out that he's really a knight at heart. You know, content to worship the princess from afar. For that, I'm even grateful. Had he really had your love it would have been quite a different matter.'

'He's a good man, Gavin,' she persisted. 'Don't harm him.'

'You're not listening, darling,' he drawled. 'In time I'm sure both of us will have his devotion. I should think devotion would be Hartley's deepest emotion.'

'I'll go crazy in a minute,' she said urgently, her two hands joined like a supplicant's between her breasts. 'What have you come for?'

'Perhaps nothing.' He was still watching her with that curious expression.

'Oh.' She was sitting on the edge of the chair and now her robe parted to show her long, beautiful legs.

'Where do you want to go for our honeymoon?' David asked dryly.

'Nowhere near water,' she said shakily. 'You might drown me.'

'Drowning you would be no fun.'

She couldn't help looking up at him, meeting his eyes, and she blushed deeply. Deep inside her the pulsing was beginning, the knife-like desire only he could arouse.

'David,' she said, as tremulous as a child, 'please don't make me afraid of you.'

He too might have slipped into a trance, because he remained silent, just staring at her.

'Miss Rainer?' Jenny had come into the room, hesitating as she discerned the strangeness in the atmosphere.

'Oh, Jenny!' Elizabeth's voice sounded considerably shocked.

'I thought Mr Courtland might want to hear me now.' The loss of confidence was pathetic.

'Of course I do.' David stood up, very tall, very lean, the harshness dropping away from his expression.

'I'm not *very* good,' Jenny whispered, somewhat desperate now when this hero-figure was going to test her.

'Please don't be nervous, Jenny.' David put his hand on her shoulder. 'You know what you're doing and how to do it, so go to it.'

Jenny gave a quick little laugh. 'Okay,' she said happily, her grey eyes huge, shining orbs. 'I'm going to play you a Chopin waltz.'

'Which one?' he confounded her by asking.

'Mr Courtland knows a good deal about classical music, Jenny,' Elizabeth told the child. 'He would know all the Waltzes.'

'Oh, in that case,' Jenny frowned very slightly, looking serious. 'It's the Waltz in C Sharp Minor.'

They all walked into the music room and David closed the door quietly.

'I feel a bit scary,' Jenny confessed.

'Just nerves,' Elizabeth answered her in a matter-of-fact voice. 'Ignore them.'

Jenny went to the piano and squirmed about on the seat for a moment until she felt quite ready, then she began to play—better, even better, than Elizabeth had heard her play before. Her adrenalin was up, the thrill of playing for an audience.

Thank God, Elizabeth thought. She won't go to pieces at the exam.

Afterwards they all had supper together, Jenny's mood so buoyant and exuberant it made Elizabeth happy to watch her. As long as I do some good in the world, she thought, my life won't be a complete failure. Jenny, given a little flattering attention, was blossoming like a plant hitherto denied nourishing. Her small face was starstruck and it took a certain amount of firmness for Elizabeth to get her off to bed.

'What are her real chances?' David asked, as he was leaving, still with no explanation for why he had come.

'Good.' The ribbon finally slid off Elizabeth's shiny hair and they both crouched down at the same moment to retrieve it.

'Here.' He was obviously deriving a perverse pleasure from his visible effect on her. She was trembling, her skin flushing, and her long hair was covering one side of her face like a golden gauze.

He brought her to her feet, the fire racing from under his fingertips along her skin. 'Let me tie it for you.'

'*Please*, David,' she said desperately.

'Two can play these dangerous games.' He was revelling in her total vulnerability, inclining her face towards him, hovering over her like a hawk. 'I thought you'd want to know the date we get married,' he said with a kind of amused triumph. 'You'll have to fit in with my plans, I'm afraid, so if you've got any concerts lined up you'd better cancel them.'

'I can't leave Jenny,' she cried.

'December, darling,' he cut off her protest. 'Jenny's exam is next week.'

'When, then?' she bowed her golden head.

'That's right. I could just do with an obedient bride. The seventh, does it suit you?'

'It will have to, won't it?' What a future lay ahead at David's brilliant mercy!

'Sure you wouldn't like to invite your uncle and aunt?'

The cruelty bit deep into her, made her hot and reckless. She brought up her hand in an imperative gesture, wanting to strike him when violence was abhorrent to her.

'No,' he smiled balefully, catching hold of her wrist.

'Don't try me too far, David,' she warned him, 'or I'll disappear.'

'Again?' he asked scornfully.

'You're hurting me!' She wanted to cry. Instead she drew in her breath sharply.

'I'm sorry.' His voice deepened in elaborate apology. He brought her hand up to his mouth and pressed his lips against the delicate tracery of veins.

She could feel herself swaying. Even her shoulders curved towards him. Praying he would stop . . . ah, *no*!

'You know, Elizabeth,' he said tautly, 'sometimes I find it impossible to accept that you jilted me. Are you really two people, or maybe three or four?'

'Sometimes,' she said hollowly, 'I think I'm no one at all.'

Elizabeth wanted to keep Jenny with her that final weekend before the exam, but Mrs Neilson insisted that Jenny go home. It must have been a disaster, because when Jenny arrived with her mother at the

Academy both of them were gravely unsmiling and Jenny's coltlike legs, one with a long scratch, were over-exposed in a green dress that was too short and of such a shade as to turn Jenny's sallow complexion to mud.

Dear God! Elizabeth thought as she went hurriedly towards them. Couldn't Jenny have worn her school uniform? At least it was of a length and it suited her.

'Hi,' Mrs Neilson said abruptly.

'Good morning, Mrs Neilson, how are you?'

'I've been better.' Mrs Neilson gave a thin smile. 'Johnny's been sick over the weekend.'

'Oh, I'm sorry. He looks such a strong boy.' Elizabeth had sighted him briefly and thought him a big bully. He had been kicking a stray dog at the time.

'He *is*,' Mrs Neilson returned in no uncertain tone. 'Some virus he caught off Dad.'

'I could have kept Jenny,' Elizabeth murmured, cursing the fact that she hadn't.

'Oh, Jenny,' Mrs Neilson shrugged her shoulders wearily, so that one might have concluded Jenny was a write-off.

'And how are *you* feeling, Jenny?' Elizabeth asked quickly, seeing with dismay that Jenny was on the brink of tears.

'Sick.' Jenny pressed her tummy.

'Almost certainly,' Mrs Neilson groaned, 'she's comin' down with something.' She put out a hand and roughly brushed back Jenny's hair that fell untidily around her shoulders.

'I think we might plait that,' said Elizabeth, taking the bit by the teeth.

'As you like,' Mrs Neilson returned shortly. 'I

don't have to wait, do I? I don't like leaving Johnny by himself.'

'No, Mrs Neilson,' Elizabeth said gravely. 'I'll bring Jenny home.'

'She can go back to school,' her mother said. 'Well, good luck, then, Jen.'

'Thanks, Mum.' Jenny turned up her face for her mother's glancing kiss.

No thanks for Elizabeth, and she didn't expect any. Even the box of groceries hadn't eventuated.

In contrast to Jenny, all the other applicants were dressed in their very best; clothes immaculately clean and pressed, shoes gleaming, hair freshly washed. They were sitting in the corridor nervously chattering to one another and Philip, Elizabeth's other star pupil, made his way towards them.

'Caroline has just gone in, Miss Rainer,' he told Elizabeth quietly, then looked at Jenny and smiled. 'Hello, you must be Jenny?'

'Yes.' Jenny heaved a sigh.

Elizabeth introduced Philip and the two young people stared at one another thoughtfully. 'One of us won't be coming back,' said Philip.

'It won't be *you*!' Jenny cried prophetically.

'Both of you have an excellent chance,' Elizabeth said softly. 'Philip, don't crack your knuckles.'

'I'm nervous.' Philip looked down at his hands—strong hands, nearly man-size at fifteen.

'Don't do it inside the examination room,' Elizabeth warned him. 'Remember you're judged on your whole performance. Would you see Roger Woodward cracking his knuckles?'

'No, Miss Rainer,' Philip grinned. 'Don't worry, I won't forget. Not after all the hard work you've put in. Mum asked for the day off, but they wouldn't give it to her. She was spitting chips. Any case, she's got something for you, from all of us.'

'Oh, Philip!'

'Something you like,' Philip told her.

'I really think he's going to win,' Jenny said as Elizabeth was plaiting her hair in the ladies' room.

'There'll be four scholarships offered,' Elizabeth said to reassure her.

'There are twenty kids outside.'

'Scholarships aren't meant to be easy, Jenny,' Elizabeth told her with a smile. 'The thing is to give it all you've got. Play from the heart. Forget the little passages that are giving you trouble. Get the *idea* across, the marvellous emotion that inspired the composer. Think of it as though they're up there watching you, depending on you to make their music live.'

'I'll try,' said Jenny, a certain constriction in her throat. 'I wanted to wear my uniform, but Mum wouldn't let me. She hates uniforms and she hates ironing the blouse.'

'Why didn't you do it yourself?' Elizabeth pleased with her efforts. The way she had plaited Jenny's hair, starting right from the front, suited her.

'Mum won't let me since I dropped the iron.'

'I think I'll put just a little bit of blusher on your cheeks,' Elizabeth decided. 'You're very pale.'

'I hate this dress,' sighed Jenny. 'Did you see what Johnny did to me? He hit me with a paling.'

'Good grief! I hope he got into trouble.' Elizabeth rummaged in her handbag for her Lancome blusher in its burgundy and gold case.

'Johnny never gets into trouble,' Jenny shrugged,

like a weary old woman. 'Mum always finds some excuse for him. According to her the paling leapt up and hit me itself. It sure hurt.'

With just the faintest dusting of the powder cream Jenny's pallor was lifted, but there was no help for the green dress. Jenny would have to win the day on her playing.

One way and another it was a nerve-racking day. Caroline came out of the examination room, told all of them she was 'dreadful' and was violently ill—mercifully not before Elizabeth rushed her to the ladies' room. That was the start of it. One of the boy violinists baulked like a horse at a fence and refused to go in to the exam, whereon his normally goodnatured mother cuffed him sharply on the ear and the blow carried the day. Only Philip seemed to emerge fully self-possessed, a true musician to his fingertips and destined to become internationally famous.

Jenny was in despair.

'I let you down,' she wailed. 'My playing was all right, but when the judges spoke to me I just *froze*!'

It was difficult to say who was the more upset, Elizabeth or the child. Where there was money these things didn't matter, but where there was none, the scholarship was all-important. Without it, Jenny's talent might be buried forever; left to wither and die. Her parents had already indicated their feelings in the matter.

Of course Elizabeth, in her position, could see the results that same afternoon, but the places were not being announced until the Wednesday. Jenny would have to agonise until then.

'About this girl Jenny Neilson.' Elvira Rubin had

called Elizabeth into her office, her plump bejewelled fingers searching for the written report. In
her heyday, thirty years before, Elvira had been a
magnificent pianist, though she had given up the
concert platform to devote her life to rearing her
four children, all fine musicians, and looking after
her more brilliant husband, the violinist, Lucien
Renault. Now Lucien was dead, but Elvira continued to rule the Academy with an iron hand.

'Yes, Madame?' Elizabeth took a seat opposite
the opulently decorated, Renaissance type desk.

'Ah, here it is!' Elvira adjusted her eye-glasses
and gazed down through the half-moons. ' "Good,
good, not so good . . . overall there was a sparkle
to the performance, a well developed technique and
a surprising insight. . . ." That was you, of course?'
Elvira challenged her. 'You put in a lot of work on
this girl.'

'She's a most deserving case, Madame.'

'So.' Elvira pursed her lavishly painted lips. 'I'll
tell you now, Elizabeth, the boy Philip is accepted.'

'Oh, marvellous!' Elizabeth was torn between
pleasure for Philip and tremendous disappointment
for Jenny. Philip had parents who were working
their fingers to the bone so their son could succeed.
Jenny—ah, Jenny!

'Now about this girl,' Elvira fixed her with still
brilliant eyes. 'Tell me something about her background. Underprivileged, no?'

For ten minutes Elizabeth talked without stopping and not once did Elvira attempt to stop her.
'So you see how it is?' Elizabeth concluded a little
lamely after so much fire.

'Are they really so bad?'

'It's just that they have little love to spare for

their daughter. It's all given to their son. I'm sure had he Jenny's gift, they would have borne all the practising far better. In fact, it might have sounded like music. As it is, they think Jenny is making an intolerable din.'

'Peasants!' Elvira muttered scathingly, her black eyes contemplative. 'I don't know that we can afford another child. Not these days, with teachers' fees so high.'

'I'd be happy to teach her for nothing,' Elizabeth said.

'Darlink, I know that,' Elvira stared Elizabeth in the face somewhat ironically. 'I would be not so happy. You are that rare thing, a performer *and* a teacher. A very fine teacher, Elizabeth. I am very pleased with you. Your time is valuable to the Academy—too valuable to waste on the little ones. The master classes, they are the thing!'

'So Jenny misses out?' For the life of her Elizabeth couldn't keep the mourning out of her voice.

'Her dress, her deportment, her speech, I understand are terrible.'

'She's a very fast learner, Madame, and she's only fourteen years old. At the mercy, you might say, of her parents.'

'I'm so grateful we have *good* ones.' Elvira smiled dryly. 'I must think about this, Elizabeth. Only I'm a genius at balancing the finances! I've called you in because I knew you would want to know. Also your pupil, the boy Philip, has scored the highest marks of all. His performance as I heard it was memorable. These are the pupils the Academy needs. I feel sure you are happy for him and for yourself.'

'Yes, Madame.' Elizabeth picked herself up out of the chair.

'On the other hand,' Elvira peered up at her, 'someone might wish to make the Academy a gift, some prominent business man. I understand Sir William Langley is one of your greatest admirers?'

'I couldn't ask him, Madame,' Elizabeth faltered, knowing Elvira would do anything for money.

'It was just a thought.' Elvira's beaky nose twitched. 'After all, a few thousand dollars would be a drop in the ocean. I'm amazed more business men don't contribute to this great cause, to put this young country, Australia, right at the very top. The potential is here. Didn't my own beloved Lucien settle in this country, found this Academy?' As always when Elvira spoke about her late husband her lips began to shake. 'They should be pleased to give!' she cried ringingly. 'Anyway, my dear, let me think about it.'

Elizabeth hadn't expected David to ring her, but he did. 'How did Jenny go?' he asked.

'Missed out,' she said drearily.

'Hell!'

'What a mixture you are, David. Or is it only me you hate?'

'You sound unhappy,' was all he answered.

'I was counting on that scholarship for Jenny. One of my other pupils was awarded the top mark, but he's had more time to develop. Also his parents adore him. They'll be ecstatic when they hear, and God bless them.'

'How much is the scholarship worth?' he asked her, and clicked his tongue when she told him. 'Isn't that rather miserable?'

'It's a big help all the same.'

His voice deepened sardonically. 'Don't sound

so shattered. Have dinner with me tonight. There
are a few details we have to discuss—like when to
tell Bill. We might even get around to discussing
Jenny.'

For David to say such a thing was almost a
commitment. She would never have found the
nerve to approach Sir William Langley, and his
philanthropic gestures were limited to what was
tax-deductible. But David was different. His family
had a tradition of helping those less fortunate than
themselves.

That evening she dressed with particular care.
Once it had been heavenly making herself beautiful
for David, now the desire was still there but mixed
with great trepidation. There could be no argument
tonight. The path had to be kept clear for Jenny.
She would be as unprovocative, as submissive as
she knew how—repentant even, but for God knew
what.

'Where are you now, Uncle Edward?' she
thought bleakly. Her own sources had confirmed
that her aunt and uncle's marriage had broken up
shortly after Jill had left them to find more excite-
ments in Sydney. Greedy, conniving, jealous little
Jill. But then she was her mother's daughter. Elizabeth had always had an affection for her uncle,
and a deep sympathy. He was a weak man, it was
true, he had never stood up for her, taken her part,
but he had never been unkind to her either, just
weak.

The pensive face that looked back at her was
very sensitively modelled. Too sensitive, she
thought. I'm more sensitive than anyone I know,
and it's not funny. Her eyes were very large and
brilliantly green, her nose short and straight, her

mouth full, a romantic mouth, she supposed.

Lately she had been toying with the idea of having her long hair cut. Of course in her career it paid her to look prodigiously arty and her usual gleaming coil kept her hair out of the way. All the same, it could look good shoulder-length. She had already arranged for Marion to have her hair styled and had promised to go with her.

'Just in case I back out!' Marion had warned her. Perhaps she could have her own crowning glory shorn at the same time. It reminded her too much of the old days, the way David used to call her his medieval princess. Ah, what it was to have one's life blighted: to have everything turn out so very differently. She was even beginning to fear her life would be disruptive from beginning to end. Her unhappy fate to which she had to surrender. Why else had David come back into her life?

Still lost in her reverie, she applied perfume to all her pulse spots, savouring the beautiful, subtle fragrance, the overtones of gardenia. The pity of it all! To be forbidden to say she loved him. For a moment she pressed her hand mutely to her breast. Remorse over Melanie was still gripping him.

Melanie. She would have tried very hard to make him a good wife. Melanie of the dark hair and dark eyes, always staring up at David with open adoration. Melanie might have expected to have a good life; that was only natural.

Elizabeth stood up quickly before desolation overtook her. Her dress was gold lace in a classic long-sleeved, V-necked design and she wore it with infinite grace. Or that was what other people saw. Elizabeth had been blamed too bitterly for her beauty for it ever to engage a sense of vanity.

'Beauty is only skin deep, my girl!' Aunt Ruth had drummed into her, beside herself with Jill's spasmodic acne.

'Your niece, not mine!' was another. 'She is nothing to me.'

As if she didn't know that from the age of seven. Odd how shockingly unkind Aunt Ruth had been, was still willing to be. It had to be Aunt Ruth who had exposed her to Angela. After five long years she still wanted to make Elizabeth suffer. Some women, it seemed, could never extend mercy.

They dined in a new restaurant Elizabeth had never been to before, and it was obviously going to be the new 'in' place because the evening glow from the table lamps illuminated quite a few well known faces.

'Are you hungry?' David asked her, his eyes scanning the menu.

'I can't remember.'

'Think,' he urged.

'Yes, I suppose I am. I'm not really sure if I had lunch.'

'That bad a day?' He paused to look at her, the innocent golden beauty he had so loved and worshipped.

'You know how it is,' she shrugged. 'Examinations are always hectic for the teacher and the pupil. I was quite upset on Jenny's account. Her mother sent her in in the most terrible dress. It was so bad it was unreal.'

'I thought the question was, could she play the piano?'

'Well, of course!' She shrugged lightly. 'But Madame Rubin sees her students as ambassadors for the Academy. They are, after all, the cream, otherwise they wouldn't get in. Then again poor little Jenny has a . . .'

'Come right out with it, a terrible twang. She's only reproducing the vowel sounds she's heard all her life. That can be corrected, the dress, deportment so on.'

'All these things take money, David,' Elizabeth pointed out.

'Exactly. Let's leave Jenny for the moment. What are you going to have?'

She picked up the scarlet and gold menu and scanned it with great deliberation. 'What are you having?'

'Would you like me to order?' he asked dryly.

At that very moment the waiter appeared at David's elbow and he proceeded to order while Elizabeth looked around her, only half seeing the distinguished decor.

In due course their Martinis arrived and David said in a very sardonic voice, 'You realise as soon as we tell Bill he'll want to arrange all sorts of parties?'

'But he can't!' She became visibly tense and her green eyes glittered. 'Have you forgotten I was engaged to Gavin? He's still with you all. I can't possibly hurt him.'

'Listen, my love, you belong to me now.'

'You know what sort of an arrangement *we* have, David.'

'Only *we* know,' he said curtly. 'As far as Bill's concerned, the rest of the world for that matter, you're my first love, my lost love.'

'You're not going to find it easy to play the part convincingly,' she said with intense emphasis. 'Even little Jenny caught the strain that's between us.'

'Aren't most lovers strained on the eve of the wedding?'

'I'm serious, David,' she said. 'Sir William is a very perceptive man. In fact he has eyes like a hawk. You won't be able to hide what's really in your mind.'

'Even hate has its own magic.'

'Oh!' She drew back. 'I can't go on with this.'

'Rubbish, Elizabeth,' he said softly, 'you know perfectly well you're bound to me.'

Which was so frighteningly true. His black eyes were sparkling at her with a kind of malign humour and she wanted to curse aloud, but she couldn't.

'Anyway, Elizabeth, you're a very good actress. I'm relying on you. When you set out to play a part, no one could be more convincing. You simply act as though you love me. Surely you haven't forgotten how?'

'I don't want parties, David,' she said. 'I don't want to be fêted and fussed over when all the time it's a cruel game.'

'I expect you'll just have to put up with it,' he responded wryly. 'Bill sees himself as family. He's absolutely smitten with you, this perfectly beautiful girl. He was quite bewildered by your choice of Hartley for a fiancé.'

'Was he?' Elizabeth said bitterly. 'I'd rather have Gavin than you and Sir William put together.'

David threw back his head in the old arrogant fashion and laughed. 'It wouldn't have worked, Elizabeth. In time, a short time, your Gavin would have driven you mad. Haven't you noticed he's a bit of an old woman?'

'You don't respect people, David,' she said angrily.

'Darling, I do when they've earned it. I'm not implying Hartley does some knitting in his spare time, but he's a very settled kind of person, sort of semi-retired. Obviously he couldn't have taken Sir William's place even if he is capable of creative work. Moreover, he's resigned to losing you, when I would want to kill you.'

'Failing that, persecution.' Elizabeth picked up her cocktail and drank it. 'Tell me, David, do you want children?'

'I want everything, Elizabeth,' he said, fixing her with a black, unwavering scrutiny. 'We're not just going to share a house. I want you completely. You're going to bear me a son. We can both love him.'

'What about a daughter?' She wasn't going to cry.

'Of course a daughter. I'll love her just as much, probably more—a little girl who looks like you. I loved you so much I wanted to know what you were like from the moment you were born. In lots of ways, I'm not cured.' His handsome mouth twisted in self-mockery. 'Try to look happier, Elizabeth, here comes the first course.'

Over coffee and liqueurs he broached the subject of Jenny again. 'How would Jenny's parents react to a handout?' he asked.

'I don't think Jenny would see it,' Elizabeth responded ironically. How the Neilsons would like to divert that money to Johnny!

'It would be arranged that way, Elizabeth,' David pointed out patiently.

'It wouldn't work,' she looked down at her ring-less hands. 'It seemed to me Mr Neilson is a man with an outsized chip on his shoulder. He might resent a gift of money to Jenny in some peculiar way. Had she won the scholarship that would have been a different matter. Anyway, all is not entirely lost. Madame Rubin is thinking over Jenny's case.'

'You mean Madame Rubin might be persuaded to let her in for a generous donation,' David said shrewdly.

'Something like that.' Elizabeth was embarrassed. 'But, David, it would be such a good cause.' Spontaneously she put out her hand and caught his wrist, her luminous eyes glowing and full of appeal.

Her skin was very white against his dark tan and her action seemed to have stunned him, for he was sitting very still looking down at their joined hands, his becoming taut under her grip. 'Such compassion!'

'I really care about Jenny,' she faltered, and withdrew her hand. 'It wouldn't be a waste of money, David, I know, given the opportunities, she can make it. She's incredibly dedicated. Far more determined than I ever was.'

'Really?' His dark, handsome face regained its hard, sceptical look. 'We wouldn't want her to turn into your kind of girl. Not that it's possible—Jenny hasn't got your fateful beauty.'

The hostility that was in him made her heart turn in her breast. Still she kept her voice soft and the appeal in her eyes. 'Please help her, David?'

'No need to sell yourself, Elizabeth,' he said with dark insolence.

It flicked at her like a whip, so she put her head down, her lashes dark and heavy against her creamy skin.

'If you're quite finished,' he said abruptly, 'we'll go.'

There was no use arguing, no use hoping, no going back either.

When he took her arm he discovered she was shaking. 'I don't understand you, Elizabeth.'

'Please, does it matter?'

He put her in the car and went around to the other side. 'Look at me.' He turned the interior light on.

She couldn't control it. The tears that had been threatening all evening glittered in her eyes.

'God,' David said violently, 'what does it all mean? You walked out on me, wrote me a letter I'm not likely to forget for a long time, left me to marry someone else in a sheer bloody rage, someone who never deserved the unhappiness I gave her, you emptied my life, now you're crying!'

'Sit it out,' she said tiredly.

'Why should I? It's all so improbable. I simply can't figure you out, Elizabeth. Nothing about you seems to add up.'

'Let's not talk, David,' she shook her head. 'There's nothing to say.'

He looked at her for a long time in silence, then he started the car, driving in complete concentration back to her apartment.

'There's no need to come up,' she told him.

'I'll see you right to the door,' he said shortly. 'My mother taught me that.'

'Did she teach you your cruelty?' Normally she would never have said that, but the wine had loosened her tongue.

'You're a fool, Elizabeth,' he said softly, 'such a fool.'

'Go ahead, hit me,' she said wearily.

'I don't think I could stand to strike a woman. Even you.'

She fled him then, her vision blurred, the hurt so unbearable she pressed a hand to her mouth to control the sobs.

'Elizabeth!' he called, not waiting for a response but coming after her.

'Go away!' She had to struggle, sick with emotion and blinded by tears.

'Please.' The outside light was shining down on them and it was evident he found it all distasteful, for he pulled her into the deep shadow of the eaves. 'Give me your key.'

'So you can keep at me?' she accused him in a frenzy. 'Is that it? So you can drive me out of my mind?'

'Darling, you lost it long ago.' Practically crushing her against him, he took her evening purse from her and withdrew the key to her apartment, listening to her agitated breathing and the little sobs she was finding it difficult to control.

Inside the apartment the moonlight showed the dark outline of furniture and Elizabeth nerved herself to break away from him before he dazzled them both with light. A little spear of pain was in her side and she was trembling violently, almost maddened by their enforced intimacy, the unimaginable hating and wanting and longing at the same time.

'Now, what's this all about?' he asked tautly, leaning back against the door and holding her forcibly to him.

'We should be avoiding one another, David, like the plague!'

'You're babbling.'

'I can't *do* it,' she cried wildly. 'This terrible pretence. I want an ordinary life.'

'Don't shout,' he said wearily.

'I'll shout if I want to! This is my apartment.'

'Then I'll let you explain when the police come to the door.'

She dropped her head, defeated, sunk in despair. 'Oh, I hate you, David!'

'No, you don't.' His hands dropped to her waist, linked like an unbreakable chain.

'I do. Anything between us is a mockery. There will always be the past, the nightmare and deception.'

'What deception?' he asked urgently. 'If you'd only tell me!' He took her head between his hands, forcing it up. 'Elizabeth?'

'There's nothing *to* tell!' She gave a drowning little laugh. 'Nothing I can tell you. Funny, isn't it?'

'Hysterical.' He shook her violently so her head on its graceful neck lolled.

'Oh—David!'

'I'm sorry . . . *sorry*.' He sounded as though her involuntary cry of pain had shocked him.

'I'm so tired.' She rested her aching brow against his shirt front.

'Why can't you talk to me?' He lowered his dark head and kissed her wet cheek so tenderly she thought she would never forget it.

'Go away, David,' she whispered, all her defences undermined.

'No. I ought to have ignored that vicious letter, come after you, whipped you if I had to, chained you to my side.'

'Please stop, *please!*' His mouth was covering

every inch of her face, save her mouth.

'If I can,' he muttered blindly, his heartbeat racing, faster and faster.

Elizabeth had to close her eyes against the tumultuous climbing hunger. 'What we had, David, was sacred. This is wrong. Unhappy, bitter. . . .' She was going rigid against his urging mouth, stunned by the intensifying pressure.

'Don't cry, Elizabeth,' he begged.

'I can't *stop* crying.' Was there any way out of this enormous craving?

'You don't have to pay for your crimes all at once,' he told her.

'Oh God!' It was useless. He would never believe in her innocence even if he couldn't leave her alone.

'I've been wanting to make love to you every minute, every hour since you walked into that room at Langley,' he told her harshly. 'You went so white I thought you were going to faint. Of course I wanted you to, I felt so wretched.'

'Stop, David, this is madness!'

'Our own special kind!' he laughed bitterly. 'And there are people who actually don't believe in fixations.'

'Oh—*stop*!' Her legs were giving way on her, so he was all but taking her full weight.

'Don't sound so tragic, darling. I'm only making love to you, a little.'

Only the beginning, yet it was awesome, the tremendous emotional response. She shook her head and the slow tears came again. Inside the apartment it was quiet, so quiet, the bright moonlight stealing across the room, the scent of the field carnations she had bought in abundance from the little fruit stall on the corner. . . .

'My lost love,' David murmured, beginning to kiss the side of her tender mouth. 'God, this is an orgy! I can taste all your tears.'

'Then pity me,' she whispered.

'That's a helluva request. I'm pitying myself. Why should one golden blonde be able to inflict all this pain? Why were you ever sent into my life? It was all worked out. I doubt if I'd ever known what it was to love someone to the point of ruin.'

'*I* didn't ruin your life,' she sighed, with the saddest profound pleasure, her own mouth trailing across the satin rasp of his skin.

'Perhaps not entirely. Mine was the greater share, the greater responsibility. No one was ever able to understand that I couldn't forget you. Melanie was so pretty and sweet and adoring. She tried so very hard.'

'Don't torture yourself, David,' she said with the deepest, heartfelt compassion.

'You're doing that!' He jerked his dark head up, suddenly staring down at her, the pearly oval of her face. 'Elizabeth, my torment, surely you did love me. *Do*. Or is deception, seduction, so natural to you you can persuade a man of anything?'

'I loved you, David,' she said poignantly, 'all those years ago.'

'Five,' he returned bleakly. 'Near to five hundred years ago. But the important thing, the all-consuming thing in your life was your career?'

'Yes.' She had a secret and she had to live with it. The events of the past were impossible to wipe away or explain.

'Well, you're very good, but you're not at the very top,' he told her.

'Perhaps I didn't really want that at all,' she said elusively. They were still standing in the almost darkness, her body full against his, yet it seemed to strike neither of them as odd.

'You're a wonderful liar.' David laughed gently, his hands skimming over her. 'You realise this time you'll never get away?'

'Yes, now I see it's to be my destiny.'

'Say it, then.'

'Say what?'

'That you'll marry me and we'll be happy ever after!' He gave a groaning laugh that held a trace of anguish.

'It's too late for that.' Elizabeth began to wipe the tears off her cheeks with the back of her fingers.

'Don't you want to sleep with me?' he asked gently.

'No.'

'Don't you want to sleep with me now? The two of us the way it used to be. Nothing can change that.'

'How strange.' She felt completely exhausted, in a dream state where it was impossible to alter anything, even the thing she dreaded and dearly wished for.

'It would be perfectly easy to take you now.'

'I suppose so,' she agreed sadly. 'You always did when you wanted to.'

'No, darling,' David corrected her. 'I waited.' He lowered his dark head and brushed the briefest kiss across her mouth. 'I waited for years, I assure you. At least until you gave away those plaits.'

'Oh——'

'What's the matter?'

The feathery kisses were sheer torture, but he was well aware of it, using that method, perversely delighting in securing her submission. 'You promised me, David,' she appealed to him, trembling with emotion.

'So I did, only you seem to want me to help you out.' His mouth came down harder this time, but as her own mouth opened up ardently under his, he pulled back, deliberately lifting his hand to switch on the light.

In an instant they were drenched in brilliance and he stared down at her, concentrating on her dreamy, dazed state, the sexual languor, the total vulnerability of her emerald eyes and pulsing mouth.

'Funny, you don't look the wicked enchantress,' he drawled mockingly. 'More like my prisoner.'

'It's a wonder that you want me.' Unsteadily she drew away from him, clicking another switch so the revealing brilliance was dulled to a golden glimmer.

'On the contrary,' he said softly, almost menacingly, 'you are *so* beautiful. I can't wait until we're married. And neither, I've had time to find out, can you.'

CHAPTER SEVEN

ON the Wednesday morning, before the results of the examinations and the issuing scholarships were posted, Elvira called Elizabeth to her large, imposing office; more a kind of library with its masses of books, pictures and bibelots, the deep comfortable seating and the somewhat overly luxurious decor.

'Sit down, my dear,' Elvira waved an imperious hand, her dark eyes blazing. 'So, where *is* it?' The perennial search, but never was there a desk more untidy! 'Aha!' she picked up a slip of paper and waved it aloft. A cheque of some kind. 'Who said the great patrons are dead!'

Elizabeth flushed deeply and resisted the impulse to have a good cry. 'May I ask how much it is, Madame?'

'No, you may not!' Elvira continued to wave the cheque gaily. 'This is what you might call a windfall. Besides, I have instructions not to tell.'

'At least you can tell me the name of the donor?'

'Certainly I can!' Elvira burst out laughing. 'It is your great friend Mr David Courtland. You know very well you asked him, naughty girl.'

'I spoke to him about Jenny, yes,' Elizabeth agreed.

'But not about the Academy?' Elvira looked affronted.

'Of course the Academy,' Elizabeth said earnestly. Surely David had made the proviso that Jenny had to be accepted.

'There's plenty for everybody,' said Elvira. 'Your little protégée and a boy, a violinist. This year we shall bring the scholarships up to six.'

'That's wonderful, Madame!'

'Yes, as you say, wonderful!' Elvira put the cheque to her mouth and kissed it, leaving an imprint of lipstick. 'Mr Courtland is unquestionably a very generous man. I have asked him to our end-of-the-year concert on Friday night. I want him to allow me to thank him personally. So far, we have only spoken to each other on the phone. He has such an exciting voice. I'm very susceptible to voices, you understand.' Elvira narrowed her eyes and went off for a few moments, while Elizabeth released a deep breath and looked down at her hands.

So Jenny was to be accepted, she thought wonderingly, and all through David. His expression had been so alarming when he had left her that she had thought he would reject all her pleas. Now she had learned that not only Jenny was to be accepted, but another deserving student as well. Of course Elvira would hold on to the bulk of it for the Academy, but they had found a way to manoeuvre around Mr and Mrs Neilson.

'May I tell Jenny myself, Madame?' Elizabeth asked when Elvira came out of her reverie. 'I doubt whether her parents will bother to ring up.'

'Of course you may!' Elvira beamed at her, softened to marshmallow. 'You know the sort of thing to say. We are awarding additional scholarships this year, the standard was so high—and indeed it was. By the same token, without this wonderful cheque it would have been impossible to take your little Jenny. She would have had to come back next year.'

Remembering how the Neilsons felt, Elizabeth was certain there would not have been a next year. Still bubbling over with happiness and pride, Elvira dismissed her, calling at the door to send in Miss Barrett. She wanted to have a 'teensy' word with her.

'What have I done now?' Vera Barrett cried, terrified.

'Nothing, I'm sure,' Elizabeth tried to soothe the nearly cowering violin teacher. 'She's in a terrific mood.'

'She *is*?' Vera stared at her, astonished.

'She is,' Elizabeth told her smilingly. 'I shouldn't be surprised if you're not going to gain an extra pupil.'

'Where from? The scholarship kids?'

Elizabeth checked an impulse to say more. She was so bubbling over herself. 'Go and see, Vera,' she said mildly. 'I promise you it's good news.'

In her own room, Elizabeth rang Mother Superior at the Convent, who literally fell to her knees to thank God, then afterwards she rang the Neilson home, received no answer, then dialled through to Mr Neilson at work.

'She *what*?' Jenny's father positively bellowed into the phone.

'Gained a place at the Academy, Mr Neilson,' Elizabeth repeated, holding the receiver away in a sheer reflex action.

'Good God!' Mr Neilson laughed until he choked.

'I knew you'd be pleased.'

'Just wait till I tell the boss. He seemed interested, would you believe?'

'It's a great distinction, Mr Neilson,' Elizabeth pointed out warmly. 'Only the most gifted students are accepted, the ones most likely to make music their career.'

'Phew!' Mr Neilson breathed into the mouth-piece explosively. 'I just can't believe it—our little Jenny! Did you hear that, Bill?' he called to someone in the background. 'Our Jen's won a scholarship to that blinkin' Academy!'

'Great!' Bill exclaimed. Elizabeth heard him quite clearly. 'In a couple of years' time she can teach my kids. The wife is always going on about music lessons.'

'Are you still there, Miss Rainer?' Mr Neilson returned to the phone. 'I know you're probably busy, but would you like to come over for tea tonight? We'll have a celebration. You might even be able to tell me how to go about building this sound-proofed room. There's room if we shift the billiard table upstairs.'

Elizabeth accepted for Jenny's sake, but in the end, it turned out very well indeed. Jenny was obviously in the seventh heaven, so much the object of her parents' attention that poor Johnny was all but left out. Having a concert pianist in the family might not be all that bad, and already a few of Mr Neilson's mates had offered to help him put up that room.

'Well, come along, then, Jenny,' Mrs Neilson prodded her daughter just as Elizabeth was leaving.

'We have a present for you, miss,' Jenny stammered. 'A big thank-you from all of us. Especially from me.' She launched herself suddenly at Elizabeth and hugged her. 'It was all your doing. Your help.'

'What about us?' her mother queried. 'Didn't we encourage you?' Mrs Neilson was quite oblivious now to her former stand.

'Well, here it is.' Jenny turned away to accept a present all wrapped up in ruby cellophane from her mother. 'I hope it's right.'

'Go on, open it,' urged Mr Neilson, like a child.

It looked like a sculpture, though it was difficult to tell which way to hold it.

'You bein' so arty and all,' Mrs Neilson explained.

'Why, it's . . . fantastic!' Elizabeth smiled at them all, beautifully disguising her true feelings. 'Thank you so much. I'll keep it always.'

It was quite true. She would keep it. But where?

They all walked down to the car with her and stood there waving her off. Unmusical they might all be, with the outstanding exception of Jenny, but they all understood success. From now on Jenny would assume her rightful place in the household. She might even rate the right sort of clothes.

The phone was ringing when Elizabeth let herself in to the quiet of her apartment. 'Where have you been?' David asked without preamble, sounding very cool and arrogant.

'At Jenny's,' she said a little desperately. 'Did you think I'd taken another lover?'

'I don't think you'll ever try.'

'Oh, David, please, I don't want to fight. I want to thank you for what you did for Jenny and for the Academy. She was so happy and excited tonight I wanted to tell her.'

'Well, you can't,' he said flatly.

'I know,' she said softly, apologetically. 'Her

parents have only just realised her worth. It was touching to see.'

'Come to think of it, so is your voice. Very touching. The way you say *David, please!*'

It was impossible to stop him. 'Madame Rubin wants you to come to the concert on Friday night,' she told him.

'There's no way I could make it. I thought I told Madame Rubin that. What I'm trying to tell *you* is, we're having dinner with Bill on Saturday night. Then we'll announce our news. We can't keep it a dark secret any longer.'

'It will make me seem so fickle ... so empty,' Elizabeth protested.

'Why should that bother you right now?'

'Goodnight, David,' she said tonelessly.

'Hang up on me and I'll come around,' he threatened.

'I could hardly be more depressed than I am right now.'

'That's how it is these days—depression, elation, wild swings of the pendulum. Just remember Bill is old-fashioned. He'll expect to see you radiant now that you've found your true love again.'

Why was he so totally in control, hanging up on *her*? Elizabeth stood in the hallway staring vaguely at her hand on the phone. Already her mind was racing along to Saturday. What she would do and say. What she would wear. Prosaic things in the face of a major upheaval. There was something obdurate about David's refusal to allow her back into his heart. It did not make her feel any better to know she was in his blood. He had even admitted he wasn't free of her and he wouldn't be satisfied until he was.

What then?

Marion was strangely reluctant to enter the highly fashionable hairdressing salon.

'It's a mistake, Elizabeth, I know it is,' she said pathetically, almost shredding her right arm with her nails.

'For goodness' sake!' Elizabeth returned indomitably, 'I've made this appointment and you're going to go through with it. We both are.'

'You too?' Marion whispered incredulously. 'Why ever would you want your beautiful hair cut?'

'I'm going to change my image,' Elizabeth said emphatically. 'I might even dress differently as well.'

'Good grief!' Marion seated herself quietly in a chair. 'Is it Gavin?' She looked at Elizabeth with sympathetic eyes.

'Not Gavin. It's somebody else these days.'

'What it is to be young!' Marion fetched up a desolate sigh, suggesting she wished to God *she* could make any number of mistakes.

Christian, who was to cut Marion's hair, came towards them. 'Hi, sweetheart!'

'But surely. . . .'

'He's talking to me, Marion.' Elizabeth had known Christian since he first swaggered on to the hairdressing scene. As a cutter and stylist he was brilliant.

'Your aunt?' Christian eyed Marion doubtfully.

'A good friend—Miss Langley.'

'Hi there, Miss Langley. Would you like to come to the basin?'

Marion stood up precipitately like someone

attempting to escape, but Elizabeth put her hand on her arm. 'I'll be right here beside you.' She could almost hear Marion's inner wails. Even Christian gave an understanding guffaw.

'Please don't worry,' he gave Marion his cheeky grin, 'the end result will be highly gratifying. I can guarantee to chop ten years off your birthdays.' Or the way you look now, he thought with a kind of shared sorrow. That anyone could wear such an embarrassing hairstyle, and really she had good hair.

Simon came exchanging good mornings and told Elizabeth she would feel a lot freer with several inches off.

'I might even change the part. I'm not sure.'

An hour and a half later, Marion was unrecognisable. The whole salon wheeled around her, hairdressers, clients, applauding Christian's genius.

Only Marion sat stunned. What had happened to her face, the sagging lines and the perpetual diffident expression? She looked different, almost young, and the gleaming highlights in her lustrous hair, a natural auburn, were wonderfully kind to her complexion. Her hair had been cut short, brushed up and away from her face, framing it beautifully, softly, creating an illusion of—yes, prettiness.

'Next, skin care!' Christian announced. 'Your approach is all wrong, though you do have a good healthy skin.'

'It's all right, Christian,' Elizabeth smiled. 'We're going shopping.'

'I can't believe it!' muttered Marion, still in a state of shock.

'Hair is the single most important part of your

appearance,' Christian lectured her. 'Why a woman
with good, thick, curly hair would choose to wear
a bun,' here he shuddered, 'I'd never know.'

'Nor me.' Marion could scarcely tear her eyes
away from her own extraordinary reflection. What
a transformation!

Make-up wasn't a problem, nor clothes. Miracles
could be accomplished on a limitless charge account. After a lifetime of repression a wide-eyed
Marion went overboard.

'It's like being a girl again!' she exclaimed.
'Young, pretty, able to attract men.'

Finally Elizabeth had to call a stop. 'We'll never
get it home.'

'Let them send it,' Marion said grandly, finding
for the first time in her life that it was glorious to
be rich. 'I never knew there were so many beautiful
materials. What about jewellery?'

'Surely you've got plenty at home?'

'I suppose so. Cases of it in the safe. The last
time I wore anything of value was 1959. I was
twenty-one at the time.'

'Leave the suit on,' Elizabeth begged her. 'You
look so elegant.'

'I do, don't I?' Marion swung on her, reverting
to her old fearful self.

'Don't lose courage, Marion,' Elizabeth urged
in her firmest voice, the one she reserved for a student about to go to pieces. 'You've got eyes. You
know you look good. Much more to the point, you
can even look better. It's all up to you. Do
you want to look attractive or do you want to go
back to——'

'Looking dreadful.' Marion interrupted. 'You
don't know Father's acid tongue. He can under-

mine my confidence in a moment. If he should say
I'm a fool. . . .'

'Then he's speaking out of malice, Marion, and
I can't believe he would.'

'You know I had a love affair once,' Marion
confided.

'Just the one?'

'His name was Anthony. Such a nice name, don't
you think?'

'Yes,' Elizabeth agreed quietly. 'What
happened?'

'Father called him a gigolo, told me I was blind.
He fell for my money, you see.'

'Did you actually know that?' Elizabeth asked.
'How was it proved?'

'Father checked him out, of course. He said
Anthony had preyed on a succession of fool
women—a terrible thought.'

'So you ended the relationship?'

'Father did,' Marion sighed. 'Strange, years later
I met Anthony and his wife—such a charming
woman. I don't know how Father found out that
Anthony was a fortune-hunter. His wife told me
quite seriously how amazed she had been when
Anthony asked her to be his wife. She was only a
secretary in his Company and she'd never known
anyone so important.'

'I'm sorry, Marion,' said Elizabeth. 'Really
sorry.'

'I'm the sort people lie to,' Marion sighed. '
should have checked.'

They loaded as many parcels as they could int
the boot of Marion's car and the rest had to
sent.

'See you on Saturday.' Elizabeth bent to k

Marion's cheek. 'David and I are having dinner at the house.'

'But Father never said one word,' Marion answered, looking positively fed up, then animated. 'You and *David*?'

'I've been meaning to tell you,' said Elizabeth. 'I knew David years ago. Didn't your father say anything?'

'To *me*?' Marion smiled deprecatingly. 'I'm one of the world's rejected women.'

'Then it's about time you got out and had a good time. All it takes is a phone call. You could get on a plane and jet around the world, stay in all the best places, meet people. The whole world's your oyster, Marion. Don't pass it up.'

'Are you inciting me to mutiny?' Marion asked straightforwardly.

'I suppose I am,' Elizabeth realised wryly.

'I think, then, I might!' Marion said finally. 'Certainly I felt in my bones there was a link between you and David. I suppose you were in love?'

'Yes.' Elizabeth's heart took a sudden lurch.

'And Nadia didn't approve of you?' Marion asked broodingly. 'I had a suspicion you were the girl in David's life. Nadia was a possessive woman extreme—a trifle unhinged, actually, when it o David. I expect she sent you about your s?'

n't want to go,' said Elizabeth quietly.

never hold out against the Nadia I re-
A mere girl measured against a woman
Well, what's the situation now?'

oing to get married.' Said out loud it mensely final, binding.

you!' Marion smiled stirringly. 'David

hasn't been happy, has he? Neither have you. Gavin is a dear man, but you and David are perfect in my view.'

'Thank you, Marion.' Elizabeth dipped her head, still unfamiliar with the free fall of her shoulder-length hair. 'I truly never wanted to deceive you.'

'I know, dear.' Marion patted her hand. 'You had your reasons.'

'Meanwhile,' Elizabeth said dryly, 'everyone is in for a few shocks.'

'Tell you what,' Marion said brightly, 'as you're totally without family I'm going to elect myself the honorary aunt. I have a new wardrobe, so now I'm going to throw a few parties. Aunts generally do when a favourite niece is to be married. Honestly, it all couldn't have happened at a better time.'

Elizabeth could hardly tell her her assumption was all wrong. She waved goodbye to Marion, then lowered her arm slowly, brooding on a future David had arranged. It was almost as though she was being hypnotised into something against her will, a travesty of a marriage with the past like some inescapable demon in their lives. David would never really forgive her no matter how long they lived together. He might want to, but then something would happen to stir everything up. How awful it was to be locked up in the past, to be prevented from telling the truth for ever. She just should have let Uncle Edward go to jail. It was his problem after all, though she was certain she would do the same thing again.

'What shall we *do*?' Aunt Ruth had cried in terror. 'The shame will kill me. How could you, Edward? How *could* you?'

But even Uncle Edward couldn't fully explain

his extraordinary compulsion. The opportunity was there and he had surrendered to an inexplicable temptation. He couldn't even believe himself that it had happened. He was just going to sit there in his chair looking prematurely old and weak and terrified, while Aunt Ruth poured contempt and revulsion on his head.

But it had all worked for Nadia Courtland. Odd how quickly she had become aware of the disappearance of the money when no one else in the store knew. Odder still how she had dealt with the matter herself, she who had nothing to do with all the minor Courtland enterprises which somehow spread over the whole town and the vast outlying district. Yes, Nadia Courtland had known, and she had known immediately, almost as though it was she who had put temptation in a weary, unhappy man's way. Or it just seemed that way.

So absorbed was Elizabeth in her thoughts that she went to step off the pavement without properly looking both ways, and the blaring horn of a passing car brought her rudely back to reality. How many times had she gone over it all before! It was about time she stopped. There was nothing to be gained, just as she couldn't run away from it. There were secrets in everybody's life, but hers had lost her the chance of happiness with the man she loved.

When David called for her on the Saturday, he reacted to her new hairstyle immediately.

'Now why did you do that?' He stopped her by catching her wrist and turning her around.

'I thought it would be easier if I created a new me.'

'Show me.' He started to walk round her.

'It was so long it took up a lot of time.' She

stopped herself just before she started apologising.

'You must see that it makes you look very glamorous?'

'Yes.' She frowned slightly. 'Actually I'm sick of looking like a Vestal Virgin.'

'I wouldn't have said that at all. I'm sorry you got your hair cut, Elizabeth. I liked it long, as you very well know, which is probably why you had it cut. Nevertheless you look beautiful either way.'

'Thank you, David, how kind.'

'Are you ready?' he asked nonchalantly. 'Bill likes everyone to be absolutely punctual, and never forget it.'

'Yes, ready.' Elizabeth had checked every aspect of her appearance a dozen times. To go with the swing of her hair she had chosen a very up-to-the-minute outfit that was rather a departure from her usual style. Mostly she wore skirts for the evening, but Sally had talked her into this particular outfit, a blouse in gold thread worn with silky black crêpe trousers. It was a Jean Muir original and because she was tall, long-legged and very slim, the whole effect was strikingly chic and arresting. It seemed to amuse David at any rate, for he looked her over with a decidedly mocking glint in his eyes.

Sir William was there to greet them when they arrived, and if Elizabeth had anticipated any difficulties they didn't arise. Eight all told sat down to dinner, all of them previously unknown to Elizabeth except by reputation, and all in all it turned into an exceptionally pleasant and comfortable evening. The surroundings were superb, the food and wine of the same order, and for once Big Business and its machinations didn't dominate the conversation.

Everyone with the exception of Elizabeth and Sir William, who had had a few days to get used to it, was dumbfounded by Marion's new image.

'Please tell me, Marion, where you go?' Elizabeth had overheard one of the women guests questioning Marion about her hairdresser, and afterwards Marion had caught Elizabeth's eye and winked. It was almost impossible to equate this elegant, trim-figured and beautifully turned out lady with the Marion of old, and under the influence of her new appearance, Marion's personality expanded. Where previously she had floundered or withheld all comment, now she was even driving her points home.

'I presume you're finished, Marion?' Sir William asked her once, briskly, but Marion didn't fall apart.

She simply nodded and flashed her father a smile; a strong, self-confident smile that made him feel vaguely uneasy. What if Marion took it into her head to run her own life? She didn't even need his money. Her mother had taken care of that.

Sir William himself set up the piano and for the usual fifteen minutes or so Elizabeth entertained his guests, combining a few of the well-known piano favourites; Chopin, Albeniz, Gershwin, the Liszt *Liebestraum*, a special request. . . .

'Splendid as always, Elizabeth!' Sir William took Elizabeth's outstretched hand and kissed it. 'Now I believe you and David have some news for me?'

David played the part of the handsome, dashing, sweep-you-off-your-feet lover to the hilt, so all that remained to Elizabeth was to look lovely and blushing and occasionally bestow on David a fond look.

'I worried so much about you with Hartley,' Sir William confided. 'A good man in many ways, but not for you. I would like you to know I couldn't be more delighted that you and David have finally come together. I know a little of the story, my dear, just as I know Nadia Courtland was the most appalling snob in the world. David tells me you've already settled on the date?'

'December the seventh.'

Sir William laughed at her. 'Whatever David settles will be perfectly all right with you, I'm sure. Would it make you happy if I gave you away?'

'It would, Sir William.' From somewhere she found a radiant smile. Those shrewd, vivid blue eyes were focused on her intently.

'Then it's done!' he responded. 'From now on you must look on me as family. David is the son I always wanted but never had.'

'Well, that's that!' David murmured as the Aston Martin slipped out of the Langley driveway. 'You did very well as the blushing bride-to-be.'

'I suppose I do have some talent as an actress.' It came out far more sarcastically than Elizabeth intended.

'Sir William to take your arm. St Mark's. You know how all the gossip columnists are going to love that. Tell me, what are you wearing?' he asked.

'I haven't thought about it,' she said shortly.

'You'd better,' he said. 'A great bond seems to have sprung up between you and Marion,' he added. 'I suppose you were responsible for her metamorphosis?'

'I merely helped out. It was all possible long ago,

but Marion, in a manner of speaking, has been hiding out.'

'She's a good girl, Marion,' David said quietly. 'She'll make you a good friend.'

At her front door he took his leave of her without so much as a pat on the shoulder. 'Goodnight, Elizabeth,' he said.

'Goodnight, David,' she responded, equally unsmilingly.

Wedding of the Year, she thought, as she tossed around on her pillow. Ha-ha!

The days ran away like sand. Elizabeth never realised she had so many friends or people who genuinely wished her well. Now she wore a ring, a beautiful emerald flanked by diamonds, and people squeezed her hand and beamed at her, always thinking she was a girl very deeply and happily in love.

'Oh, you're lucky! He's absolutely *marvellous*!' Sally had enthused. 'You're going to have the most wonderful marriage, but please, *please*, always stay my friend.'

That promise was easy, but Elizabeth couldn't possibly discuss her coming marriage with anyone. The parties, the little afternoons went on. She was showered with gifts, magnificent ones from the wealthy and the ones she liked just as much from the families of her students. On every side she was told what a very lucky girl she was, when she had never had a speck of luck in her life.

A few days before the wedding, the anonymous letters began to come. 'My God!' Elizabeth murmured, white with shock.

Marion, who had come over to have coffee with her, jumped up. 'What's wrong?'

Elizabeth shook her head slowly.

'Tell me, dear.' Marion put a hand on her arm.

'An anonymous letter, that's all.'

'Show me,' Marion said sternly, sounding like, of all people, her father.

'I can't show you, Marion.' Elizabeth crumpled up the page in agitation before Marion snatched it away. 'It's too unpleasant.'

'How vile!' Marion, too, had lost her colour. 'Someone who wants to hurt you?'

'Someone who knows exactly how to do it.'

'My dear girl, sit down,' Marion urged. 'You look very upset. Why don't you let David handle this? He'll get to the truth of the matter and confront this *person*.'

'I'm not having David upset,' Elizabeth cried, and it was true she was trying to protect him.

'Haven't you a clue who wrote it?' Marion persisted.

'Someone who hates me.'

'Who could hate *you*?' Marion's soft voice was tinged with disbelief. 'Are you sure it's not just a crank? You and David have been getting plenty of publicity. David is an important man in his own right, and there's Father as well. I mean, he gets threats every week. It's this crazy world we live in—the violence, and nobody knows what it's all about.'

'Forget it, Marion.' Elizabeth tore the grubby sheet into a thousand pieces. 'I will.'

Of course she didn't, and another letter arrived the following day. Elizabeth hurried upstairs to read it, her hands trembling in agitation. It had to be Aunt Ruth, Jill—surely not Uncle Edward. Who else would know the whole sorry story? Who else would want to destroy her? Why didn't they simply

sign their name? She clutched blindly at the arm of
a **c**hair and slumped into it. So they were going to
give the papers the facts? What were they? That
once her uncle had embezzled money from the
Courtlands. That Nadia Courtland had spared him
for a price. She couldn't bear to re-read the dis-
torted details. What an unpleasant story it made!
How much more unpleasant and sensational it
could be made to look in one of the lesser
papers.

In the end, because she couldn't think of anyone
else to talk to, she called Gavin. Gavin had assured
her he would always be her friend.

'You must tell Courtland,' he told her in a slow,
ponderous voice. 'He'll know what to do. Buy them
off. I take it they're your relations?'

'Who else could it be?' Elizabeth exclaimed. 'Oh,
Gavin,' she sighed sadly.

'Dearest girl!' he sprang up and put his arm
around her. 'I beg of you, tell Courtland. I
wouldn't care to cross him myself.'

'Then he would have to know all the facts,'
Elizabeth told him. 'His mother's part.'

'However painful, he must hear,' Gavin insisted.

'Can't you do anything for me, Gavin?' Elizabeth appealed to him, and immediately he began
to bluster.

'B-but what *can* I do? I mean, I'd do anything if
I could. Such an unpleasant business. I'm sure I
don't know what Sir William will say.'

'Can't we find out if Uncle Edward is alive? It
will harm *him*.'

'It will, of course.' Gavin frowned and gave
Elizabeth a level look. 'Don't think Angie has
anything to do with this.'

'I really hadn't thought of her,' Elizabeth assured him.

'It's true,' Gavin said musingly, 'she had some correspondence with your aunt. She still lives, apparently, in your old house. But why would *she* seek to rake up the sordid past? I mean, it was her husband!'

'She may want to hurt me more than she cares about herself. Or it could be Jill.'

'Well, you can't sit there moping,' said Gavin, peering into her pale, still face. 'Take my advice and tell Courtland. He's the best man for the job.'

Ten minutes later Elizabeth found herself confronted by an icily angry fiancé.

'What the devil was Hartley doing here?' he demanded.

'He just dropped in to say hello.'

'I don't want to see him here again!'

'I can't avoid my friends, David,' she said broodingly, 'even for you.'

'You've got to be kidding.' He picked up an empty tumbler that had had Scotch in it and put it down again distastefully. 'From now on you can ignore Hartley except at social functions.'

'Can I ignore you too, I wonder?' The sun was going down and she switched on a light.

'If it's going to make you feel a little less trapped.'

Elizabeth wanted to laugh wildly, because she was always walking into some trap or other.

'What's the matter?' David asked abruptly, his black eyes daunting.

'Nothing.' She brushed one side of her hair back.

'I don't believe you.' He came to her, his strong

fingers forcing her head up. 'You're very pale—why?'

'I have an awful headache.'

'I *know* you, Elizabeth,' he said threateningly.

'And you can't ever trust me to tell the truth.'

'Is something worrying you? Something I should know about?'

'What would you care!' she sighed in weak despair. 'I'm tired, that's all, David. Too many parties. Too many people telling me how wonderfully fortunate I am to have the great David Courtland sweep me off my feet.'

'You're about to cry,' he accused her.

'I told you, I'm *tired*.'

Incredibly he put his arms around her waist and drew her to him. 'You evidently have something to hide.'

'I've always had something to hide,' she whispered bleakly.

He didn't answer and because she was so nervily distraught she laid her head along his hard chest like a child seeking comfort. 'Hold me, David,' she begged him. 'Just hold me and don't talk.'

He did more. He lifted her in his arms and walked back to the sofa, cradling her against him, his manner, the way he held her so exquisitely gentle it might have been the David of long ago.

Then they were together and he was stroking the hair away from her face. 'In two days' time you'll be my wife.'

'I'm so tired, David.'

He continued to stroke her head. 'Tell me what you ever did that my mother got such a hold over you?'

'Oh God, David!' She closed her eyes and gritted

her teeth, still with her head pressed against his shoulder.

'So she paid you a lot of money. What did you do?'

'I fell in love with her son,' she said slowly. 'I did love you, David. I loved you so much. My only lover. You've finished me for anyone else.'

'All right, I accept that.' His hand moved to her nape. 'I'd like you to tell me the truth—the whole truth.'

'Wasn't it all in that letter?'

'The one bloody thing that nearly drove me out of my mind. It made me so mad I wanted to kill you. I couldn't even accept that you'd written it, something so almost obscene. For a while I really did go mad, but there was always my mother to lean on. She'd known all along what you were really like.'

'So you decided you'd never loved me at all.'

'Oh, come, darling,' he said sardonically,' we both know there's the most peculiar bond between us. Why else are we getting married?'

'Not for love.'

'Whatever.' He tipped her head back and looked at her.

'Kiss me,' she said with a kind of tired entreaty. 'You don't even seem to want to kiss me any more.'

'For a good reason.' He stared down into her shadowed eyes.

'Well, I need you to,' she said in despair.

'And what if I can't stop?'

'But you're different now. You told me so.'

His hold on her tightened, but she needed the pain. 'You can't possibly know,' he said tautly.

'David?' She put up her arm and encircled his neck. 'Can't we pretend we've just discovered each other?'

'All right, I don't mind.' His arms were nearly crushing her. 'You're fourteen, is that right?'

'No.' There was a shadow of frenzy in her face. 'Be kind.'

'*Kind?* God!' His reaction came fast, so fast she barely glimpsed the flame in his eyes.

An iron control snapped like a twig and he scooped her up and carried her through to her room.

'*David!*' Everything was moving too fast, the feverish intensity moving from him to her. She saw the way he was looking at her, the wariness, the fleeting shadow of hostility, and beyond and above everything the sheer force of desire.

Her dress slithered to the floor and his arms closed around her hard, bearing them both down.

'David,' she said, and her voice was unbearably brokenhearted.

'My love.' His mouth moved over her temples, her closed eyes, the curve of her cheek and under her chin. Moments that should be ecstasy clouded with threats from the malevolent past. 'What's wrong?'

'I'm afraid.'

'So help me, so am I.' He lowered his mouth to the vale between her breasts and she held his head there, desperately clutching at the unwilling tenderness in his voice. His wonderful voice, velvety, vibrant, but often possessed of a cold, cutting edge.

They lay there together quite still for a long time as though each was in truth too frightened to move or speak. 'I love you,' Elizabeth said tentatively, her hand in his hair.

'Do you?' He lifted his head to smile at her, but it was a smile that hurt. 'What does your love mean, Elizabeth? The right to your beautiful body. I want much more than that.'

'You're insatiable,' she whispered, so he had to bend his head to hear her words.

'And you're my only vice.'

'Ah, David, how can you say that?' Her eyes shimmered with tears.

'I've hurt you. How odd!'

'Perhaps you're hurting yourself?'

'Surely it's the same thing.' With his hands on her shoulders he put his mouth to her breast, and if he had been looking at her in that moment he would have seen all her love for him shining out of her eyes.

'You're so sweet you make me desperate!' His voice came to her out of a whirlpool of powerful sensations. '*Why*, Elizabeth? Why the betrayal?'

'I wish . . .' she sighed.

'This can't be a game—is it?'

'Don't you know what happens to me when you touch me?'

'I want to know what goes on inside this delicate skull.' He cupped his hands tightly around her head. 'What goes on inside your head? What impulses come to you that turn you into somebody else?'

'*David.*' She said his name and fell silent, though the pressure of his fingers was making her temples begin to throb.

'Your bones are so fragile I could crush you,' he muttered.

'You're making me feel odd.'

'Separate from your body?'

She closed her eyes, dazed, and as her lids came down so did his mouth. It expressed anger and a futile rage, then, when she offered no resistance, a deeply human hunger.

Desolation went rapidly to the most perfect physical communion, a fantasy of the senses where there was no room for bitterness or reproach. As soon as they came together, in an incredibly short time, their bodies spoke for them. Tenderness, a rapturous passion, something very precious. Even—love.

'I used to dream about this,' David muttered. 'All the time. Your white skin and your slender bones, the way you so perfectly fit my hands.'

It took all her strength to tell him, but it was very important, the source of their tragedy, but she could only tell him so much.

'David, I must speak to you.' She turned her head aside so his kisses fell on the creamy column of her neck.

'Not now. I only want to love you.' His dark, olive skin was faintly flushed and his black eyes were brilliant.

'It's so important.'

'All right,' he laughed shortly and rose on his elbow. 'You're going to confess your sins, is that it? Ask for my absolution? You've got it. You've got it all.'

His hand was still cupped around her breast and she put her own hand over his. 'For the past few days I've been getting letters in the mail. Not the usual best wishes, ugly ones, cruel and full of malice.'

'Where are they?' His face paled and every

muscle tautened. He looked, in an instant, hard and forbidding.

'I tore them up.' In fact she had only torn up the one.

'You *what*?' He looked down at her incredulously. 'You should have given them to me at once.'

'I didn't want you to suffer as well.' Her voice shook.

'Tell me what they said.' The dark face was charged with menace.

'No. Oh, no, no, *no*!' She made a frightened sound and swung away on her side, loath to meet that formidable stare.

'Tell me.' He caught the point of her shoulder, though she tried to huddle into the mound of pillows. 'From the start.'

The ghost of Nadia Courtland was suddenly in the room, a handsome, glittering ghost, smiling triumphantly because she knew the extent of Elizabeth's dilemma. How could she injure David's mother without injuring herself? How could she begin to blacken the name of the woman David had adored? His own mother, the woman who had idolised him from birth.

'I'm waiting, Elizabeth,' he said harshly. 'I want you to turn back to me and compose yourself. There are no letters now, remember? You destroyed them. I have to hear it from your own honeyed mouth.'

She turned slowly, seeing the turbulence that was gathering in him like a terrible storm. One hand sought her slip as a kind of protection, but he restrained her.

'Leave it,' he said tightly. 'God knows I know

what you look like.'

'Yes.' She could only lie there, her golden hair in complete disorder, sheening all over the pillow. 'I think it's from Aunt Ruth, or maybe even Jill,' she began raggedly. 'No one else would know so much.'

'Hell!' David interrupted violently, his tone contemptuous. 'How could *they* possibly do us damage? Two miserable, vindictive women. If you're sure it *is* they, I'll pay them a surprise visit.'

'You may need to,' Elizabeth said unhappily. 'They threaten to release certain information to the newspapers.'

'Like what?' He sounded disgusted, not even hostile.

'Like your mother gave me money to go away to Germany.'

'Germany?' He looked down into her eyes.

That was a slip, a bad one. She had never meant to say that. So far as David knew she had done most of her study in London.

'Would you mind saying that again?' He leaned over her, both of his palms pinning her body.

'I spent some time in Germany,' she faltered.

'How much time?' With his winged eyebrows forked he looked watchful to the point of danger.

'It's a long story, David.'

'I'm sure it is,' his eyes narrowed sardonically while he drank in the sight of her. 'That's the whole trouble. All your stories are so involved and they all seem to centre around letters. Tell me, darling, is this some pathetic plan to get away from me? Because if so, it won't work.' He bent over her and kissed her mouth hard. His beautiful shirt was open to the waist and she could see his powerful rib cage and the dark matting of hair.

'Please, David.' She put out her hand caressingly, moving it gently back and forth across his skin.

'Sorry, kiddo, it won't work.' He pulled himself to his feet and rebuttoned his shirt, his long tanned fingers steady and precise. 'I know your dear aunt detested you because you were so beautiful and ambitious, but I can't accept this sort of thing. What could she possibly say? Who the hell cares, for that matter? If my mother gave you money, so what? Even a lot of money. Over the years my family have been pretty generous to a lot of people.'

'There are a few things you don't know, David,' she said, and drew in her breath.

'Then you'd better tell me.' His handsome mouth twisted, but not in a smile. 'Stop being so mysterious, and dredge up some facts.'

Elizabeth sat up and lifted back her tumbled hair, unaware that the simple action lifted her exquisite breasts.

'Beautiful!' he said dryly. 'You're a miracle.'

'Hand me my robe,' she asked.

'No. I like to look at you.' He sat down again on the side of the bed, black eyes glinting, ready to caress her again.

'You'll have to do something,' she said wildly.

'You can say that again.' He put his hands on her shoulders.

'David, you have to speak to them without delay. You may be able to face them and come out the victor. I know *I* can't.'

'Hell!' he shook his head as though he had taken a heavy blow. 'You know, Elizabeth, you're not only the most beautiful, most talented, most seductive woman I'm ever likely to know, you're also the most interesting. You make a fine psychiatric study. Tell me, are these impulses uncontrollable?'

'*Listen!*' She tossed her head fretfully. 'I can't be entirely frank with you. Just warn Aunt Ruth or Jill or whoever off. You can do it.'

'But you're not giving me nearly enough information,' he said jeeringly. 'Now *you* listen, my golden-haired darling, there is no way you're going to slip away from me. This wedding is going through. I don't give a damn if there *are* vicious letters. They can make them all public if they like. It's you I want. I could never get tired of you. One never knows what you're going to do next.'

'The letters will be released, David,' she said more quietly, her green eyes steady on his. 'They'll hurt you in lots of ways, and I don't want to be around when that happens.'

'Ah, now we get to it,' he said broodingly. 'Try anything, my love, and you'll be sorry, I promise you. There's nowhere you can run this time. You've done it before, but you'll never do it again. You can't even begin to know how very unpleasant I can get.'

'I'm not going anywhere, David,' she whispered.

'Good.' He stood up, lean and ruthless, worlds away from the rapturous lover. 'In two days' time you and I have a date together. I wouldn't want to miss it for the world.'

The next morning, her mouth dry with apprehension, Elizabeth waited for the postman. Whatever detestable things were going to come out she had twenty-four hours to stop it. She had money saved.

She had already rung the bank. Aunt Ruth and Jill had always been greedy. If it turned out to be neither of them, all was lost.

She heard the sound of the postman's whistle coming up the street, but when she flew down to the box a tall form materialised and grasped her flying figure around the waist.

'David, you startled me!' Her heart rocked with shock.

'Dear me!' He looked down at her as though she were more than a little crazy. 'Let's wait together, shall we? Not there in the sun. You're already a little touched.'

'Good morning!' the postman greeted them sprightly. 'Only a few bills today, miss. And oh, another one of them funny letters.'

'Just a child.' David gave him a charming, reassuring smile. 'I'll take them. Lovely day!'

'Beautiful! A man should be out fishing. Cheerio.'

Elizabeth felt so frightened she began to shake. 'Please, David, that mail belongs to me.'

'You can have the bills.' He passed them to her, his eyes on the dingy envelope, the scrawling block letters. 'Not your handiwork so far as I can see. A city postmark.'

He walked her up the stairs with his hand at her elbow rather forcibly. 'Sit down, Elizabeth,' he said offhandedly when they were inside the quiet apartment.

'There hardly seems another thing I can do.' She subsided into an armchair while David stood in the middle of the living room and read the letter, undistracted by her anguished little sighs, reading it for a long time, over and over. His black brows

met over his eyes and his chiselled bone structure
had never been more pronounced.

'David?' she asked finally. She felt very frightened, her arms clasped around her trembling knees.

For a moment he looked at her as though he
didn't see her, a muscle working beside his mouth.
'How long were you going to continue to protect
everyone but yourself?'

'I only care about you, David,' she said.

My God! His voice was rife with a terrible disillusionment.

'Give it to me!' She jumped up and seized the
letter, feeling the heat of shock and disgust in her
face and in her neck. 'This is even more vile.'

'And stupid—mercifully. One should never
demand money.' He took the letter from her nerve-
less hands.

'I thought I could protect you,' she said
brokenly.

'I don't need protecting, Elizabeth. You do.' He
groaned and put out his arm, pulling her unresist-
ing body against him while she clung. 'You sweet
little fool!'

'It's a terrible story, isn't it?'

'The most terrible part is how *you* were made to
suffer. You were so young, Elizabeth—too young.
If you'd only told me!'

'Please understand,' she begged him.

'I don't. I can't believe it.'

'I love you, David,' she exclaimed.

'Why you *should*, astonishes me.'

'Anything that hurts you, hurts me.'

'God,' he said again, resting his chin on the top
of her head. 'You didn't write that monstrosity of
a letter either.'

'Forget about it,' she begged.

'What kind of human being would write that? My own mother? That beautiful, elegant, worldly woman? Do you know how many times I wanted to strangle you because of that letter? *You*, the other half of me. By far the better half. My dearest, only love.'

'But no one was to know that, David,' she said sadly. 'You said yourself no one understood what we meant to each other—the abiding, unquenchable love. Your mother considered she was doing the right thing.'

'How very odd!'

The break in his voice affected her violently. She put her arms around his tall, lean figure and hugged him as tightly, as fiercely as she could. 'I love you, David,' she said. 'I've been loving you for so long it's possible I'm mad with it. I won't have anything spoiling it for us now—not the past, not your mother, not Aunt Ruth or Jill or whoever it is. We're going to be together the way it was meant. Ordained, if you like. I'm not going to let you hold on to the old wretchedness. If I can forgive and forget so can you. We've got to start afresh, David. We've *got* to!'

'Darling!' He even laughed a little at her furious insistence. Her emerald eyes were blazing and the wild rose colour had mounted to her cheeks. She looked beautiful, invincible and passionately alive. 'Will you just allow me to say, *forgive me*?'

'No.' She shook her head.

'Please.' David tilted up her chin.

'Not until we've taken care of those letters. I have another one tucked away in a drawer.'

'I thought you might,' he murmured dryly.
'There's so little time.'
'Enough,' he said briefly. 'Believe me.'

CHAPTER EIGHT

PHOTOGRAPHS of the wedding found their way into all the newspapers and leading women's magazines, and a few perfectly beautiful shots were included on the evening's television. Anyone interested, and there were many, could have scanned the papers from top to bottom, back to front, and found not one jarring word about the Courtland–Rainer wedding. Good wishes were lavished upon them, dozens of congratulatory telegrams, and a vast number of beautiful presents. Only Elizabeth's cousin Jill, who had entangled herself so briefly, recoiled from the media's offerings with perfect horror. She had been taught a lesson, one that had been delivered without an ounce of pity. It was highly unlikely she would ever resort to blackmail again.

The wedding day was held in the heat of summer under a kingfisher blue sky, and the dresses of the women guests were so deliciously cool and pretty they looked as if the beautiful, picturesque old church was entirely decorated with flowers. The bride's two attendants wore rose-pink and daffodil yellow and the bride a wonderful soft gold. All of them wore picture hats of the same fluid gold and they carried exquisite bouquets of orchids, gardenias and stephanotis.

'What artistry!' Angela cried to Gavin, quite forgetting the hostility she had once borne for the lovely bride. It was not clear what Gavin said, nor what he felt, for he was very aware of the public nature of his role.

Sir William Langley with the radiant bride on his arm had never seemed so distinguished nor so approachable, and he was seen to pat his daughter's arm comfortingly while the bridal couple solemnly exchanged their vows.

The reception was held at Bellewood, a mark of the young couple's privileged position, and it all passed like a glorious dream. It was impossible to take one's eyes off the bride. She looked so incandescent, her happiness settled on everyone, so the whole atmosphere was permeated by the celebration of love.

'Happy, my dear?' Gavin came to her, his eyes resting on her very gently.

'I'm happy, Gavin,' she said softly. 'Very happy.'

'Yes, of course. You two were meant for each other.'

Who could deny it? No one who had seen them exchange their bridal kiss that day.

It was finally time to leave, everyone crowding around them, Jenny in the lovely daffodil dress she was to keep all her life, tears standing in her huge, starry eyes, Sally, excited, laughing and crying at once, yet it was Marion who caught the bride's bouquet, laughing so gaily she looked beguilingly young.

The first night they were to spend at David's penthouse apartment, then they were to fly to Honolulu in the morning on the first leg of their honeymoon trip that was to take them through the United States, Canada and most of Europe.

'Alone at last!' said David after they entered his

apartment. 'Elizabeth!' he pulled her to him and kissed her deeply.

'I feel a little giddy,' she said when he finally let her go.

'The champagne?'

'No.' She smiled at him and it was untrammelled bliss.

'My love.' He looked down into her face and saw the clear reflection of his own desire. He lifted her easily and carried her through to the bedroom.

'Undress me.' She smiled at him, dazzling him, 'and all the while I want you to tell me how much you love me.'

'It might take a very long time.' He began with her beautiful Italian shoes, drawing her slender feet into his hands.

'Oh—hurry,' she begged faintly.

'Okay,' his answering smile was devastating. 'I love you, I love you, I've never stopped loving you.'

Her clothes seemed to melt away, yet he was unbearably gentle and slow.

'Darling,' she said ardently, staring upward at the ceiling, 'you're really very slow.'

'I'm enjoying myself, that's why.' His mouth came down on her, soft, feathery kisses, trailing everywhere, all the time in the world.

'You wretch!'

He laughed in his throat, then sobered, his black eyes searching her soul. 'With my body I thee worship.'

Her eyes filled with tears and her lovely face looked all the more remarkable. 'That was like a lightning flash,' she said shakily. 'A moment when you looked exactly like the very first time we met.

So gloriously confident, so new to life you could conquer the world.'

'I could for you, love.'

Love.

They were together. His arms closed around her yearning body, smooth as ivory, warm as silk. Peace. Security. The most wonderful partnership in the world. Two people, one flesh.

'You are so beautiful,' he said.

FRÉDÉRIC CHOPIN AND GEORGE SAND

Elizabeth Rainer, the heroine of *Broken Rhapsody,* is a concert pianist, and certainly the great piano works of Frédéric Chopin form part of her repertoire. Chopin, born in 1810 to an aristocratic Polish family, was one of the most important composers of the nineteenth century.

Renowned for his beautiful and complex piano pieces, the handsome Chopin was also famous for his tempestuous love affair with a well-known Frenchwoman, author George Sand. He first caught sight of Sand in 1836 at the house of a friend. She was wearing a Turkish harem costume and had bound her thick dark hair with a red silk scarf. Chopin was immediately taken with this exotic, uninhibited woman who had dared to write novels and articles advocating free love—a most controversial subject in the prim nineteenth century! By 1838 the couple were living together, and for the next ten years Chopin and Sand divided their time between Paris and Nohant, a small rural estate to the south. Theirs was a stormy relationship; more than once Chopin left his willful mistress, only to return and humbly beg her forgiveness.

By 1846, Chopin was beginning to show signs of tuberculosis. As he grew weaker, his passion waned, and the couple became friends rather than lovers. In 1849, Frédéric Chopin died—but his love for George Sand has not been forgotten, and his stirring musical compositions continue to touch the hearts of music lovers.

Legacy of PASSION

BY CATHERINE KAY

A love story begun long ago comes full circle...

Venice, 1819: Contessa Allegra di Rienzi, young, innocent, unhappily married. She gave her love to Lord Byron—scandalous, irresistible English poet. Their brief, tempestuous affair left her with a shattered heart, a few poignant mementos—and a daughter he never knew about.

Boston, today: Allegra Brent, modern, independent, restless. She learned the secret of her great-great-great-grandmother and journeyed to Venice to find the di Rienzi heirs. There she met the handsome, cynical, blood-stirring Conte Renaldo di Rienzi, and like her ancestor before her, recklessly, hopelessly lost her heart.

Take these
4 best-selling novels
FREE

Yes! Four sophisticated, contemporary love stories by four world-famous authors of romance FREE, as your introduction to the Harlequin Presents subscription plan. Thrill to **Anne Mather**'s passionate story BORN OUT OF LOVE, set in the Caribbean.... Travel to darkest Africa in **Violet Winspear**'s TIME OF THE TEMPTRESS....Let **Charlotte Lamb** take you to the fascinating world of London's Fleet Street in MAN'S WORLD.... Discover beautiful Greece in **Sally Wentworth**'s moving romance SAY HELLO TO YESTERDAY.

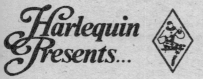

Harlequin Presents...

The very finest in romance fiction

Join the millions of avid Harlequin readers all over the world who delight in the magic of a really exciting novel. EIGHT great NEW titles published EACH MONTH! Each month you will get to know exciting, interesting, true-to-life people .... You'll be swept to distant lands you've dreamed of visiting .... Intrigue, adventure, romance, and the destiny of many lives will thrill you through each Harlequin Presents novel.

Get all the latest books before they're sold out!

As a Harlequin subscriber you actually receive your personal copies of the latest Presents novels immediately after they come off the press, so you're sure of getting all 8 each month.

Cancel your subscription whenever you wish!

You don't have to buy any minimum number of books. Whenever you decide to stop your subscription just let us know and we'll cancel all further shipments.